STAMP TWICE FOR MURDER

BY THE SAME AUTHOR

Almost Like Sisters
Angel on Skis
Boy Next Door
The Country Cousin
Jenny Kimura
Joyride
Mystery in the Museum
Mystery of the Emerald Buddha
Mystery on Safari
Ruffles and Drums
Runaway Voyage
Spice Island Mystery
A Time for Tenderness

STAMP TWICE FOR MURDER

BETTY CAVANNA

William Morrow and Company
New York 1981

 Inquiries should be addressed to William Morrow and Company, Inc., 105 Madison Ave., New York, N.Y. 10016.

Printed in the United States of America.

3 4 5 6 7 8 9 10

Library of Congress Cataloging in Publication Data

Cavanna, Betty, 1909–

Stamp twice for murder.

Summary: Mysterious events are set in motion when a sixteen-year-old American girl and her family come to France to claim their legacy of an abandoned country cottage.

[1. Mystery and detective stories. 2. France–Fiction] I. Title.

PZ7.C286Sr [Fic] 81–8291

ISBN 0–688–00700–7 AACR2

ISBN 0–688–00701–5 (lib. bdg.)

STAMP TWICE FOR MURDER

1

Through the lush fields of Burgundy the narrow road swooped and curved with the grace of a barn swallow. Riding in the back seat of the small rented Fiat, Jan felt slightly queasy. The French drivers passing the car seemed to be in an outrageous hurry. Those approaching were determined not to give ground by an inch.

Determined to outgrow her childish motion sickness, Jan leaned forward to read the Fiat's speedometer. Eighty-five! "Take it easy, Dad," she begged.

"Remember, Jan, these are kilometers, not miles," said her father. "Divide eighty-five in half, then add a little. Unless," he added, "you want to be exact."

Tony, slouched on the seat beside her, shifted his glance from the rolling landscape to his sister's face. "Chicken?" he asked in thirteen-year-old one-upmanship.

"Oh, shut up," said Jan without rancor, as her mother turned from the front seat to smile ecstatically. "Have you ever seen anything as glorious as this countryside?"

"It's OK," admitted Tony, "but when are we going to get there?"

Feeling increasingly nauseated, Jan merely smiled. (Even in station wagons she had qualms about riding in back seats.)

From the moment her father had turned off the crowded toll road heading south, time had started to drag. As anxious as Tony to get there, but unwilling to admit it, Jan kept her eyes off the road and tried to concentrate on the cottage in Vezelay, the hill town toward which they were heading.

"My legacy," Mrs. Nelson called the house willed to her by an elderly French uncle whom she had never seen. Margot Nelson's one link to her mother's French family was her middle name Frechette, so she and the rest of the Nelsons were astonished to learn that she had become Armand Frechette's last living relative and, therefore, his heir.

For months, the Nelsons had been talking about this trip to France. Jan weighed the excitement of a first trip abroad against her spot on the junior team at the tennis club and decided she could bear missing the summer tournaments. Tony gave up camp willingly. Mr. Nelson, a high-school history teacher in Moorestown, New Jersey, was free to travel during vacation, but he was frankly worried about the cost of air fare and car rental.

"It's more than we can afford, Margot. We ought to sell the place for whatever we can get," he suggested sensibly, and Jan knew he was looking ahead to the college bills he would have to pay all too soon.

"Sell it sight unseen?" Mrs. Nelson's eyes flashed at the very suggestion. "Besides, Doug, think what it would mean to the children to spend a summer in France." Her eyes grew dreamy. "Not as tourists traveling around in buses, but in our own house!" Looking deceptively fragile, she raised her arms in a buoyant gesture.

Mr. Nelson groaned, knowing when he was beaten.

"Besides," his wife continued, "we can borrow the money, if necessary, and pay back the loan from the proceeds of the sale."

"Hey, Mom's talking sense," put in Tony, and whether he had been right or wrong they finally had decided to take the trip.

This afternoon, as they approached Vezelay, Jan couldn't help but share the sense of anticipation radiated by her mother, who sat with clasped hands, approving each field of waving grain, each green hill, each stream and farmhouse. "Lovely," she kept repeating. "Isn't it lovely, Doug?"

Jan often felt like a pale imitation of her mother, whose enthusiasm was so contagious that it spread through the family. The only known fact about the cottage was that it lay in a cherry orchard, but otherwise it was a surprise package, and each Nelson had a different vision of what it would be like.

Jan suspected that her mother's was the most romantic. After all, it was *her* legacy, and she was bound to hope that it would exceed her expectations.

Tony, Jan was sure, hoped there would be a stable, even horses, although he never expressed such wishful thinking aloud.

Her father was more difficult to read. When he slowed down in the small villages that lined the road like a chain of oblong beads, he seemed to be studying the architecture. Plaster over stone, capped with red-tiled roofs, the houses stood cheek by jowl, presenting blank faces to the street, although leafy branches of tall trees sometimes promised hidden gardens. Such row houses, however, were far removed from the cottage in the cherry orchard Jan could see in her mind's eye.

Her thoughts were influenced by schoolbook pictures of Anne Hathaway's cottage near Stratford-on-Avon, rose-covered, thatch-roofed, nestled on a country lane. Although aware that Burgundy cottages were bound to be different, she had reluctantly given up that romantic thatch for tile only in the last few miles. She kept hoping for roses, however, because she wanted the cottage to be pretty and welcoming. She wanted her mother to fall in love with the place at first sight, even if she was forced to sell it at summer's end.

The road bridged a stream, broad and rippling. Ducks waddled along the grassy shore. A cottage just like the one that Jan was imagining lay behind a low stone wall in the distance. There were no roses; instead, poppies, red as the stripes in the American flag and as small as rose petals, sprinkled an adjacent field.

Mr. Nelson braked at the bridge and glanced in either direction. "This must be the Cure," he said, "the river that runs close to Vezelay." He enjoyed maps and had discovered the name weeks ago. "You pronounce it Koor."

Tony mouthed the word silently, then got to what interested him. "How close to Vezelay?" he asked.

His parents glanced at one another, smiling.

"Close enough for you to sit up and take notice," Mr. Nelson said. "You don't want to miss the first sight of the basilica."

Tony raised himself by a couple of vertebrae. "Is that a castle, Dad?"

"It's a big church, stupid," said Jan with quick superiority. "You saw the picture."

Tony settled down again, yawning, but his father's teaching instinct was aroused. "It's Romanesque, very early, twelfth century. The Second Crusade started from here."

Mrs. Nelson put a hand gently on his arm. "Save it until later, dear," she advised.

"Koor," Tony said unexpectedly. "Sounds like a birdcall."

"That's *coo-ee,*" muttered Jan.

"Much you know," Tony retorted. "I'll tell you one thing, Jan. Bet I learn more French than you do within a week." He had an ear for languages that neither his mother nor his sister shared.

"I'm sure you'll be a sensation," Jan said, while her mother sighed.

"Stop bickering, you two," ordered Mr. Nelson. "Sometimes, Janice, you act as if you were still Tony's age."

The insult stung. Although only three years older than her brother, Jan felt that they were worlds apart. Tony was just a kid. An attractive kid, however, Jan was ready to admit. He was ebullient and outgoing, with dimples that puckered when he smiled. Tony despised the dimples, because he considered them girlish. In fact, he was big for his age and sufficiently brawny to seem thoroughly masculine.

As the road ahead began to climb in slow spirals, Mr. Nelson shifted to third and Tony sat up again. Swinging through a green forest with tall trees crowding the borders beside the macadam, the Fiat emerged on a ridge with a sweeping view.

There, in the distance, was Vezelay, rising like a mirage from a spreading valley checkered with fields of ripening wheat and barley. Mrs. Nelson gave a gasp of pleasure and put her hands to her cheeks.

Summer-soft clouds like dollops of whipped cream, far from threatening, hovered over the conical hill. The sun shone brightly with no hint of menace, glancing off the tawny limestone walls of a huge rectangular building crouched on the blunted hilltop. From this distance, the village looked like an illustration from a fairy tale.

Her father pulled off the road at the first vantage point and turned off the ignition. "This has got to be one of the most spectacular views I've ever seen," he said.

Nobody had to be invited to get out of the car. Jan filled her eyes with the sight, lifting her brown hair from the back of her neck as she shivered pleasurably. Tony said "Wow!" three times, then ran around the car to stand by his mother. "Pretty nifty, huh?" He telescoped his fingers and peered through them, clowning. "Like a pitcher postcard."

Mrs. Nelson smiled, hugged him, then called to her husband. "Come on, Doug! I can't wait." Settled once more in the car, she said, "The orchard is near the top of the hill, north of the basilica. That's the side we're coming in on, isn't it?"

"More or less. But if there's a road up, it doesn't show from here."

Indeed, the only road approaching the village was the one the car was traveling on. Curving in a wide arc around the hill, it led into a paved square. On the left lay a long, low hotel, with a sign proclaiming its name, the Lion d'Or. Bright flower beds flanked a broad terrace, where fluttering lavender tablecloths covered small tables. People were sitting at many of them, sipping drinks or reading guide books. The scene was like a colored photograph from a travel folder.

Mrs. Nelson quickly spotted the tourist office, not much bigger than a double phone booth, which handily lay next door. "That's where we're to pick up the key to the house, Doug! I've got the lawyer's letter in my purse."

Mr. Nelson pulled up sharply, and the entire family, restless and eager to reach their destination, piled out of the car and into the minuscule office. A middle-aged woman with a beaked nose and graying hair finished explaining a local map to another customer, then turned to the Americans and asked, in careful English, "What can I do for you?"

Ready to try out his modest French, Mr. Nelson was slightly taken aback. "We've come for a key," he said, "that was left here by a lawyer—an *avocat*—from Avallon."

The woman took an envelope from a locked drawer and handed it over with a nod, then watched as he extracted an old-fashioned key nearly five inches long that looked more suited to a barn door than a house. "Will you sign here, please?" she asked, placing a printed form on the counter and offering a ball-point pen.

"You should sign, Margot. It's your house." Mr. Nelson stepped aside with a smile.

"Vraiment?" The clerk lapsed into French, then quickly recovered. "You plan to stay there? At the house in the cherry orchard?"

Mrs. Nelson nodded happily. "For the rest of the summer," she replied with a lilt in her voice. Then she bent her head and swiftly scrawled her signature.

A disturbed expression appeared in the woman's eyes. "You are very brave, *madame,*" she said, gravely picking up the receipt.

"What a curious remark," murmured Mrs. Nelson, as she walked back to the car. "I wonder what she could have meant by it?"

Mr. Nelson chuckled, unperturbed. "Most French working people think all Americans are rich and should stay where they belong, in expensive hotels."

"Nevertheless—"

"Maybe we've got spooks in the cottage," suggested Tony airily.

"Bats would be more like it," Jan told him.

"Oh, stop it!" her mother cried. "You're spoiling my fun." Her eyes were riveted on the road up the hill, which looked almost perpendicular. "Do you think we should walk, Doug?" she asked anxiously.

"If I stay in first gear I think I can make it," he answered teasingly. Clearly he wasn't worried about driving up any street that permitted automobile traffic. Tanned and fit-looking in his knit sport shirt, with a few threads of gray in his dark hair, he seemed quite capable of meeting the challenge.

Sidewalks so narrow that two people couldn't walk abreast lined either side of the narrow roadway. Houses and shops jostled one another. *Épicerie,* Jan read. *Charcuterie, Patisserie.* Jan couldn't pronounce the names and could only guess at their meanings, but she recognized the post office at once and noticed a shop selling postcards and a one-room restaurant. Halfway up the hill, where the ascending street veered to the right, there was a café with tables daringly set out on a triangular piece of macadam.

"Is this the only street?" Tony asked.

"One goes up, one down, from this point on," replied his mother, who was consulting a hand-drawn map she had taken from the pocket of her jacket. "We go all the way to the top, Doug, then turn left in the square fronting on the basilica."

While her father dodged tourists, motorcycles, and a delivery truck Jan clung to the back of his seat.

"Neat work," she breathed in relief, as he shifted into second in the upper square. Souvenir shops abounded, and visitors who had made it to the top on foot looked pleased with themselves.

The basilica loomed ahead in all its Romanesque splendor, but Jan gave it scarcely a glance as her father turned left and drove past it. "Now what, Margot?" he asked.

"See that wall straight ahead? Turn left again, dear. There should be a cobbled lane, with an arch over it. Oops, here it is! Back up, Doug. Let's park and lock the car. We can come for the luggage later." She brandished her key joyfully.

As usual, Tony raced ahead until he was recalled by his father. "Come back here! That's not fair. Your mother deserves the first glimpse of her dream house."

"Stop teasing me, Doug!" Then, clutching her elbows, Mrs. Nelson admitted, "I'm actually trembling!"

Together, Tony and his mother led the way along the lane, past a door in the wall (locked, Tony discovered) and a fenced kitchen garden at the back of a tall house opposite. They reached a rutted cart track for which the wall was a dead end and turned to follow it downhill. After a brief stretch, they came to a sagging gate opening on a wilderness of weeds.

"This can't be it." Mrs. Nelson stopped and studied her map again. "It can't be! Where's the house?"

Through a tangle of vine-covered trees, Jan could barely distinguish a patch of red tile. Then her heart sank, because the trees were hung with occasional bunches of ripening cherries.

"My little house in the cherry orchard," her mother sometimes called it, using the one fact they all knew to describe it.

Frozen with dismay, Jan stared at her mother's head bent over the map. She couldn't bear breaking the news and let Tony do it for her.

"Hey, look, you guys, cherries!"

Without seeing his mother's stricken face, he attacked the gate, pulling and pushing at the confining brambles. Edging through, he brandished an imaginary sword. "Attack, men! I'll lead the charge!"

He didn't lead it far. Within a few feet, he was wrapped in a coccoon of menacing thorns and ropy grapevines. He could neither advance nor retreat.

Nobody tried to extricate him. Jan and her father both stood without speaking, looking at the triangle of dark red roof. Trying to find a word of comfort, for herself as well as for her husband and children, Mrs. Nelson finally said weakly, "Of course, the orchard has been terribly neglected, but the house may be quite nice when we get there." Then, rallying, she essayed a smile. "Doug, did we bring the hedge shears, by any chance?"

A voice from somewhere behind Jan—a youthful American voice!—spoke in amusement. "It's not as bad as it looks. There's a path of sorts. If you're anxious to see the old house, I'll give you a hand."

Jan turned to look up at a tall young man with amber-colored eyes and shaggy blond hair. He was wearing faded blue jeans and a turtleneck, and he had a nice smile.

"Would you? That would be very kind!" Mrs. Nelson was saying.

Immediately the boy dropped the bicycle he had been pushing uphill into the roadside weeds. Then, crossing to Jan's parents, he introduced himself. "I'm Eric Stockton," he said.

"Douglas Nelson," replied Jan's father, holding out his hand. "My wife, Margot, my daughter, Janice. The youngest member of the family is Tony, who seems to be wound up like a kitten in a ball of yarn."

"Yarn, my eye," yelped Tony. "These thorns hurt!"

Eric reached into his back pocket and pulled out a pair of small garden clippers as though he had come prepared for just such an emergency. He moved toward Tony carefully, stamping the brambles underfoot as he went. "Stand still," he ordered compassionately. "Don't move until I've cut you loose."

Quickly Eric's competent hands clipped at the harness of grapevine. Freed, Tony stood picking off the thorns clinging to his bare arms. "Gee, thanks," he said gratefully.

Eric went on clipping the barrier vines along a narrow path he seemed to sense rather than see. With strong thrusts of his arms, he parted the dense tangle and came to an arbor with comparatively clear ground underneath. Only then did he turn back toward the gate. "I think you can make it now."

Mrs. Nelson went ahead, showing her nervousness with thanks that were too profuse. Jan followed slowly with the rest of the family, filled with foreboding. How could her mother bear it if only disappointment lay ahead?

From a turn in the path where the arbor started, a small, square house became visible. Still snipping at grapevines and pushing them out of the way, Eric led the Nelsons toward a weatherbeaten door flanked by two long windows.

"Very Charles Addams," Jan's father said, trying to lighten the chilling reality.

Eric grinned briefly but appreciatively. "The house isn't much to see, actually. Just a square box with four rooms. Of course," he added rather sadly, "nobody has lived here for more than thirty years."

"Thirty years?" Jan and her mother gasped simultaneously.

Eric nodded. "The owner went to Paris and never

came back. French villagers can be very superstitious," he added, then glanced at his watch and gave a short whistle. "Excuse me," he said. "I'm running late." As he spoke, he started toward the gate, pausing only to call over his shoulder, "Nice to meet you folks. Have a good trip."

2

"French villagers can be very superstitious."

Superstitious about what? Jan wondered, but Eric's departure was too quick for questions. He hadn't noticed the key in Mrs. Nelson's closed hand. Otherwise, Jan suspected, he might not have been in such a hurry.

The key fitted the antique lock and turned with surprising ease, but the old door sagged on its hinges. The combined efforts of Tony and his father were needed finally to force it open.

Even before she got close enough to peer inside the house, Jan was assaulted by an ominous stench that seemed to be compounded of mold and filth. No window or door had been opened for years, but something more must have caused such a foul odor. What could it be?

Her mother, gagging, backed away from the doorstep, but Tony poked his head inside a dim room veiled in cobwebs and filled with debris.

"Smells like rats," he muttered, wrinkling his nose in disgust. Quickly he emerged into the open air.

Gathering courage, Jan followed her father across the threshold. Trying to hold her breath, she surveyed a scene of chaotic disorder. Disintegrating clothing, moth-eaten blankets, bed pillows spilling feathers, and a jumble of books and newspapers had been flung helter-skelter about the room. Drawers were ripped from tables, cupboard doors stood open, and a great many spiders had led very busy lives.

Mr. Nelson made a quick survey of the incredible mess, then turned back to the door. "Well, Margot, here's your dream house," he said bitterly.

The reality was too much to face, particularly late in the day after a long, tension-building drive from Paris in a pint-sized car. Mrs. Nelson burst into tears.

Jan moved to put an arm around her mother's shoulders. "That was a mean thing to say, Dad!"

"I feel mean," her father admitted. "I feel mean and tired and hungry, and I need a shower and a drink. Come on, Margot. Let's see if the hotel can put us up for a night or two. Then we can decide how to dispose of this albatross."

"We could burn the house down and collect the insurance," suggested Tony.

"What insurance? Son, you'd better stay out of this."

Jan could tell from the flat tone of her father's voice that his anger and discouragement lay very deep. He dragged the door shut and strode ahead, kicking viciously at a piece of grapevine that had curled around his foot.

"Mother, don't cry. It's not your *fault*!" Jan did her best to be comforting, although she was very close to tears herself.

"I'm sorry." Finding some tissues in her jacket pocket, Mrs. Nelson blew her nose vigorously, but the tears would not stop. "It's just that I wanted—I wanted it to be nice and simple and—and wonderful, for all of us."

Jan steered her mother toward the gate and the arched lane that led to the car. "Of course you did. So did I. We're both too romantic, I guess."

Mrs. Nelson dabbed at her eyes and sniffled, then took a long breath.

A slender woman, with fluffy beige hair, wide-set brown eyes, and tanned skin, she looked as attractive as ever, but her special life-loving quality was thoroughly subdued. "Don't be nice to me. I'll start crying again." She broke into a run. "Hurry, darling. Dad's so mad he's apt to go off without us."

"Never!" Jan called after her, but she wasn't sure.

Her cautious, practical father had been against this project from the beginning, and now—too late—he had been proven right. The property should have been sold for whatever it would bring. Then her mother could have harbored her daydream for the rest of her life.

The Fiat, engine running, was waiting where it had been parked. Tony was sitting in the front seat beside his father, so Jan and her mother got in the back. Nobody spoke as they edged down the steep street, now crowded with people and cars. Villagers were carrying long loaves of bread under their arms, and tourists surrounded the postcard racks. Cats streaked across the road, and dogs sniffed along the gutters. When the flower-decked terrace of the hotel came into view, Jan sighed involuntarily. She had never seen a place look so cheerful and welcoming, although it was small solace.

Mr. Nelson pulled into the parking lot and spoke tersely. "Let's go see what's available, Margot. You kids stay here."

"Wow, he's really sore," said Tony, when his parents were out of earshot.

"He has a right to be," Jan replied. "We're in a monumental mess."

"That cottage is the mess. Nobody's going to pay a hundred bucks for it."

"Don't be too sure. The land is worth something."

Jan was trying to think of some way they might escape the predicament without being too badly hurt.

Tony leaned back against the car door, stretched his legs, and parked his sneakers on the steering wheel. "This bus was built for midgets," he said idly, then stirred and sat up. "I don't suppose there's a hamburger joint around here?"

In spite of her growing concern, Jan chuckled. "Go one block over and turn to the left. You'll find a McDonald's."

"There's a McDonald's in Paris," said Tony. "I saw the ad in a magazine."

From the rear window Jan could see her parents crossing the cobbled courtyard, heading back toward the car. They did not look happy, and she could guess the reason. A couple of rooms in this posh hotel probably cost a small fortune.

Tony climbed out, ready to help with the luggage, but Mrs. Nelson shook her head. "No room at the inn," she explained with a valiant smile. "The man at the desk was nice, though. And helpful. Wasn't he, Doug?"

Mr. Nelson grunted.

Speaking to Jan and Tony, Mrs. Nelson continued, "He says in the summer the balloonists stay here and everything is booked for weeks in advance."

"Balloonists?" Tony was immediately interested.

"Groups of people who like to take balloon trips," his mother explained.

"Gee, that'd be neat, Mom. Do you s'pose—"

Mr. Nelson held his head. "God help me!"

"Anyway," Mrs. Nelson said, raising her voice in determination to be heard, "the desk clerk gave us an address to try. It's not a hotel, just a house run by some Franciscan nuns—nursing Sisters—up near the church."

"We're going to spend the night in a convent?" Tony's voice cracked alarmingly. "Me and Dad too? They'll take *men*?"

"It isn't a convent," his mother said. "It's called the Center—"

"The Centre de la Madeleine," Mr. Nelson said in French. He sounded grouchy but no longer furious.

"Will they feed us?" Tony asked. His stomach was beginning to rumble audibly.

"I very much doubt it." His father pulled a five-franc piece from his pocket. "Run up the hill to the nearest bakery and ask for a *baguette*. That'll keep starvation at bay. We'll pick you up on the way, if you're quick."

"Otherwise—"

"Otherwise, there's only one way to go." With a forefinger he pointed upward.

Tony loped off with a loose-jointed coltishness that seemed very American. He was waiting on the narrow sidewalk when the Fiat crept up the hill, but he looked irritated. Chucking a long loaf into his sister's lap, he complained to his father, "Hey, you didn't tell me all I'd get was *bread*!"

"Break off a piece, and hand it to me."

"Without butter?"

"That's the way the French eat it, and they seem to survive."

The bread was restorative. Jan broke off a piece for herself and found it was very good, warm and crusty and fragrant. "Mm," she murmured appreciatively.

By the time the car crawled into the upper square, the loaf was almost gone and everyone seemed less edgy. The traffic had thinned to a trickle, and the light from the west promised a beautiful evening. If we can find a place to sleep, Jan thought, we might even have a little fun.

"You tackle the nuns, Margot. I'm going to stretch my legs a bit," said Mr. Nelson.

"Me too," said Tony in a men-should-stick-together tone of voice.

Jan and her mother walked a few steps downhill to the spot where the hotel clerk had drawn a big X on his diagram. "Suppose none of the Sisters speaks English?" Jan asked.

"One thing at a time," replied her mother, as they reached a wrought-iron gate set into a high wall. Beyond was a big stone house, three stories tall, fronting on a pebbled courtyard. A drying rack holding half a dozen dish towels stood where the last of the sun would hit it. Otherwise, there wasn't a flower or a tree. To Jan, the prospect looked uniformly gray and forbidding.

Mrs. Nelson tried the latch, but the gate was locked. She found a bell pull and gave it a tweak, which resulted in a distant jangle. After a few minutes, the door of the house opened and a tall, heavyset woman came down the steps and across the courtyard to the gate. Instead of a coif and a habit, which Jan had expected, she wore a simple cotton dress and a white scarf pinned decorously to conceal her hair.

"Bon soir," she said pleasantly, but without emphasis.

"Good evening," Mrs. Nelson said. "We need a place to spend a night or two, my family and I. The hotel is full. We were told you might be able to take us in."

The nun shook her head.

Jan's heart sank until she realized that the gesture was not one of refusal but of dismay. *"Un moment, s'il vous plaît,"* she said, and turned away.

Her progress back to the house was equally deliberate, but she returned quite soon with a short, bouncy nun who had a freckled face and a friendly smile. As she unlocked the gate she said, "I have studied English. My name is Sister Agatha. What can I do for you?"

Mrs. Nelson explained her family's predicament in simple terms. Meanwhile, Sister Agatha began to look dubious. "You have inquired the hotels in Avallon, no?"

"No," Mrs. Nelson was forced to admit.

"Avallon is a bigger place, only fifteen kilometers from here."

"You see, I own a house in Vezelay. We had expected to stay there, but it is impossible, Sister Agatha."

"Why impossible?"

"If you could see it, you'd understand," Mrs. Nelson told the nun desperately. "It's the house in the cherry orchard, at the top of the hill, to the left of the basilica."

"The house in the cherry orchard!" Sister Agatha clasped her small, work-worn hands in consternation. "Oh, no!"

Mrs. Nelson nodded ruefully. "I received it as a legacy from an elderly uncle, Armand Frechette."

Seeing the situation in a new light, Sister Agatha's manner changed. "We have a few small rooms we sometimes rent to young people or elderly travelers who are in need," she said. "Scouts, hikers, bicyclists, mostly. The rooms are *very* plain and small."

"That wouldn't matter," said Mrs. Nelson hopefully.

"There are how many persons."

"Four. My husband, my son, and this is my daughter, Janice."

Sister Agatha acknowledged Jan's presence with a polite nod, then turned back to Mrs. Nelson. "If you could manage with two rooms? There are only cot beds, two in each."

"We could manage with anything!"

"The charge is fifteen francs a person for a night. No meals, just a *petit déjeuner.*"

"We're very grateful that you will take us in," said Mrs. Nelson with sincere appreciation.

Twenty minutes later Jan and Mrs. Nelson were installed in a cell-like room while Tony and Mr. Nelson occupied its twin next door. Between the two was an eight-foot-high board wall, so flimsy that the Nelsons could chat back and forth without raising their voices. Each room was furnished with two narrow cots, a single chair, a shelf, and a bare electric bulb hanging by a cord. Nobody complained, but Jan had the temerity to whisper, "Aren't the reading lights divine?"

"Sh!" cautioned her mother with a twinkle in her eye. "We're very lucky."

"It's sure a lot better than a haystack," was Tony's opinion, expressed as the family trooped downhill on foot in search of a place to eat. "Wait till I tell the boys at school I slept in a nunnery."

"It's not even a convent," his mother murmured patiently. "It's just a resting place for tired pilgrims, like us."

They stopped to read a bill of fare outside one of the two small restaurants the village offered. Mr. Nelson blessed the law that required all restaurateurs to include prices on their menus, because the cost of four simple meals was daunting, even to Jan and Tony.

"Why don't we have a picnic?" Mrs. Nelson suggested.

"Hey! Let's!" Tony shouted. Then he added impetuously, "We could eat in the cherry orchard, under the grape arbor."

"Not a bad idea," said his father. "The stores stay open late here, and it will be light until nearly nine o'clock."

Tony was sent for another *baguette,* Jan for cheese and country *pâté,* which looked like a rather solid meat loaf. Mrs. Nelson found tomatoes, fruit, paper napkins, and plastic picnic glasses at the *épicerie,* while her husband went to the café and bought two cokes and a bottle of red wine, from which he thoughtfully had the cork drawn. Reassembling, the family set off on the rue des Écoles, which branched off from the café and led almost directly to the cherry orchard.

Uncharacteristically, Tony hung back. "Hey, Dad,

you said that sign with the bar across it means you can't enter."

"Vehicles can't enter, but people can. Even so, we'd better look out for cars coming toward us."

Along the way, however, all was quiet. The tourists had departed, and although it was not yet the eight o'clock dinner hour, the village seemed to be dozing. Apparently the French valued their privacy, because the shutters were already closed on every window the Nelsons passed.

The gate to the cherry orchard still stood ajar, and a fading sunset glow in the western sky rested tenderly on the tangled trees. Squatting at the foot of the arbor, the square little house hid its disreputable interior.

Mr. Nelson had bought a newspaper. Spread out on the ground, it served both as a place to sit and a place to put the food. With the pocket knife he usually carried, he cut the tomatoes in wedges, hacked the cheese into pieces, then left the knife sticking upright in the *pâté*. "Dinner is served," he announced.

Relieved, Jan began to relax. If her father had recovered his good humor, all was bound to be more or less right with the family and the world.

By unspoken consent, everyone spoke softly, and the picnic took on the quality of a secret gathering. Jan felt like an interloper in this strange, secluded spot, and she suspected the others shared the same feeling. That her mother actually owned the ground on which they sat didn't seem to count for a thing.

The food tasted wonderful. Everyone except Mrs. Nelson ate heartily. She nibbled at the cheese, sipped her wine, and stared thoughtfully up at a sickle moon riding in the darkening sky. Then she turned to consider the shadowy house.

"I don't care," she said unexpectedly.

"Don't care what?" asked Jan.

"I don't care if the house *is* a horror. The outside could be lovely, and it's ours, Doug. We're going to clean it out and stay here, the way we planned."

In spite of his father's groan, Tony bounced up and down in enthusiasm. "It'll be like camp."

"Or a communal pad. Have you thought about beds, Margot?"

"If the beds are hopeless, we can buy Army cots."

Her husband groaned again.

"There's water and electricity," Mrs. Nelson hurried on. "The deed says so."

"Does the deed mention a bathroom? If it does, I can't wait to see it."

"Suppose there isn't a bathroom? There's got to be an outhouse of some kind. Doug, where's your sporting spirit?"

"I lost it in Vietnam."

"Oh, honey, please! Consider the idea seriously.

We could get dozens of big plastic trash bags—the French must have *something* that's equivalent—and cart all the stuff to the dump."

"This is the dump, love."

"Doug, listen!"

"Listen!" echoed Tony in a whisper, but he wasn't looking at his father. He had swung around to stare toward the house.

With a shiver of apprehension, Jan whispered back, "Listen to what?"

"I heard something. Honest. Around at the side."

"Well, Tony, let's take a look." Mr. Nelson sounded unperturbed. He got to his feet a trifle stiffly and started toward the house. Tony followed while Jan and her mother sat still and kept quiet. Aside from a donkey braying mournfully in the distance, they couldn't hear a sound.

In the fading light, Mrs. Nelson looked bemused, and Jan could tell that she was still busily planning. Unalarmed either by the vague warnings of the villagers or Tony's unexpected whisper, she intended to persevere.

Whenever her mother set a straight course, Jan knew she was bound to be pulled along. For better or worse, her guess was that the family would be spending the rest of the summer here.

Then, from a few yards away, came a sudden crash. "Who's there?" Jan's father called in a loud voice. The only answer was a heavy thud. A dead branch torn loose from a tree? Twigs snapped, the sound growing fainter as Jan listened. Then, once more, all was quiet.

In a few seconds Mr. Nelson returned. "No use," he was saying to Tony. "I'd need a machete to cut through that jungle. Besides, it was probably just an animal. Could have been a goat or a big raccoon."

"That was no goat or raccoon," insisted Tony with a snort. He came up to stand by his father's shoulder and looked him in the eye. "Animals don't swear!"

3

Sister Agatha welcomed the Nelsons back to the Centre and locked the door behind them. Jan didn't have to accommodate her tired body to the hard mattress or the coarse cotton sheets. She fell asleep almost immediately, then awakened hours later to pitch darkness and the sound of her father's gentle snoring from the next room.

She turned and lay on her back, hands clasped behind her head, and thought about the strange day, starting so hopefully and ending so inauspiciously. Without Eric's timely help it would have been disastrous.

Eric Stockton. An American name with a hint of

Norse background. In repose, his face seemed almost sad. She wondered why.

At that moment, from somewhere nearby and far up, a clock began to chime with soft, musical, bell-like notes that sounded like a blessing on the village and on Jan herself. She lay and counted to twelve. Then she shut her eyes and once more drifted off to sleep.

Two nuns bearing trays knocked at the bedroom doors at six thirty the next morning, when it was barely dawn. Simultaneously Jan and Tony groaned. Mrs. Nelson, however, was awake and stirring. She poured *café au lait* for Jan and herself, then spread coarse black bread with a generous spoonful from a pot of homemade jam.

"No orange juice? No butter?" Tony complained from next door.

"You're in Vezelay, not on Main Street," his father said.

"Good morning, boys!" called Mrs. Nelson cheerfully. "Remember to put on your oldest clothes."

"My oldest clothes are back home," Tony reminded his mother.

"Your next-to-oldest then." This morning she was dauntless.

Sister Agatha was wetting down the pebbles in the courtyard when the Nelsons emerged. She greeted them with kindliness and agreed to let them have the rooms for another night or two, until they could do a rough cleaning job on the cottage. "The man who brings our winter firewood might prune your cherry trees," she suggested in her tentative English, indicating that his price would be fair if he could have the trimmings. "He may not be willing to work there, but I can ask."

"Please do," Jan's father said.

Aside from its indisputable state of decay, Jan wondered what else about the Frechette cottage put people off. What could have happened there to make the villagers fear and avoid it? Not even Eric had offered a clue.

While her mother took Tony off shopping for supplies, Jan and her father went reluctantly back to the house. "Let's storm the defenses and open all the windows," Jan proposed. "All those we can reach, that is."

"Or all those that will open." Jan's father was willing to try but far from sanguine. "I wonder how long I can hold my breath."

He found out, very shortly, that it was only long enough to unwedge the two front casements. Then he rushed outside, gulping fresh air, and stood with Jan under the grape arbor. "Your mother," he said conversationally, "is a damn fool."

Jan chuckled. "You might as well roll with the punches, Dad. We're in for it."

They stood together companionably for several minutes, listening to the mockingbirds singing experimentally in the trees. The morning was cool, the leaves dew-spangled. If only they didn't have to attack that wretched house!

"Ready, get set, go!" said Jan finally. "Come on, Dad."

The open windows helped, but still they were only able to spend five minutes or so heaving debris through the door. A miasma of choking dust arose that affected Jan like poison gas. When she could scarcely breathe, she staggered outside and collapsed against one of the frail supports of the arbor.

"Let's go home to Moorestown," she proposed.

"Suits me," said her father. His craggy face had lost color and his mouth was grim. After a few breaths of fresh air, however, he began to recuperate. "Once more into the fray, dear girl!" He even managed to grin.

On this expedition, he fought his way across the room and reached a window next to a corner fireplace fitted with a round-bellied black stove. The latch turned and the casements flew open without sticking. "Cross ventilation should do the trick!"

"My father the optimist," Jan muttered. She was tugging at a bundle of crumbling, yellowed newspapers when the string tying them broke in her hand. "Everything's either stinking or rotten," she said, stating the obvious.

As she shoved the bundle through the door Tony

came hurtling along the path, armed with a broom and a big box. "Cleaning equipment," he called.

"You're a day too early," Jan called back. "All we need this morning is a couple of hundred trash bags. Got any?"

"Coming right up." Tony put the box on the ground and opened a cardboard carton, extracting a blue plastic bag and shaking it out with a flourish. "Want me to give you a hand?"

"Two hands," said his father from inside the house. "Let's get a little teamwork going."

Jan held the bag open while Tony helped stuff it with trash, most of it moldy and moth-eaten men's clothing–overcoats, suits, undershirts, and woolen long johns. By the time Mrs. Nelson arrived, they had filled four bags. An hour later nine more were lined up outside.

When there was no more room under the arbor, Tony and his father carried the bags, one by one, up to the road, propping them along the sagging fence. After they had tied them with wired tape, Tony called them dead soldiers, but Jan thought they looked neat and harmless. No whiff of their contents drifted down through the orchard, and for this blessing she gave heartfelt thanks.

By now the front room was cleared sufficiently to disclose a square oak table and five cane-seated chairs, a Victorian cupboard that filled an entire wall, and an easy chair with tufts of stuffing poking through the faded chintz upholstery. Dust lay thick on everything, and the walls were a dirty gray. "What color do you think they were originally?" asked Jan.

Nobody answered.

The next room to be tackled was the kitchen, also on the front of the house. Hung with cobwebs and furnished with a big iron cooking stove, a soapstone slab and a pump, it was as forbidding as the first room but not quite so smelly. Rats and mice had feasted on the contents of overturned tins and glass jars, which, long ago, must have been dragged from shelves and scattered pell-mell on the tiled floor. There were broken dishes, rusted pots, but here and there a bucket, pan, or spoon that Mrs. Nelson deemed salvageable.

Gradually she accumulated a small hoard of objects on the stove top. Tony picked up the bucket, placed it under the pump, and was delighted when a stream of clear water rewarded his efforts. "Hey, look at that, will you!"

"Where's the sink?" Jan asked, as she swept broken crockery into a pile.

"I don't think there is one." For the first time today, her mother sounded disheartened. "There's a drain in that sloping piece of soapstone, but it doesn't seem to lead anywhere."

"Then how can we wash dishes?"

"In a dishpan, I suppose."

"And what do we do with the dirty water?"

"I don't know. Throw it outside? It might kill the weeds."

"Let's use paper plates," suggested Tony. "Then there won't be any dishes to wash. Say, that'll be neat."

As if the lack of a sink wasn't enough, Jan was looking at the stove in consternation. "We've got to heat water somehow. Do you suppose that thing works?"

"I don't know, I don't know, I don't know," sang her mother. "Ask your father, Jan. And if he knows whether it burns coal or wood, I'll be surprised."

"It burns wood," said Mr. Nelson, who had come down from the road for another bag of trash. "And it undoubtedly needs repair." He leaned on the sill of the open window. "I wonder if the person or persons responsible for this crazy mess found what they were looking for."

Jan had been wondering the same thing. What could it be? she pondered. "So far we haven't turned up a thing of any value at all."

"I have!" Tony crowed suddenly. "Look, Dad, just what you've been waiting for." He brought a rusty but intact pair of long-handled clippers over to the window. "How can we sharpen them up?"

"I've got just the thing." Mrs. Nelson went over to her booty on the stove and came back with an old-fashioned grinding stone. "The sort my grandmother used for sharpening knives," she said.

The minute she handed the stone over, Tony and his father retreated with them. Cutting back the bushes that smothered the walls of the house was a job that showed quicker results then working inside.

"There *is* an outhouse," called Mr. Nelson from a newly cleared area.

"Where's Tony?" Jan called back. "We could use him in here." There was only one pair of clippers, after all.

Tony, it seemed, had simply disappeared. Nobody was surprised, because at home the same thing happened frequently. His attention span was short, and he was gregarious to a fault. Jan suspected that he had slipped down to the Lion d'Or to see if he could get a glimpse of a balloonist in the flesh. She was also sure that before many days passed he would have a string of acquaintances in the village.

By the time he came back, Jan and her mother had dragged three more bags of trash out the front door and swept a pile of dirt into a corner. "We'll paint the kitchen first. After it's scrubbed, of course." Mrs. Nelson looked thoughtful. "We'll have to find a way to heat some water."

"And cook some food," Jan added. "We can't eat cheese and bread and cold cuts forever."

"No, I suppose we can't. Although they're nourishing." Hearing Tony's voice outside, Jan's mother went to a window and called, "Come on, you two. The noon whistle just blew. Quitting time!"

There was no noon whistle in Vezelay, but the clock with the beautiful chimes was again striking twelve as the Nelsons went up the path to the road, each dragging still another blue trash bag, filled almost to bursting.

A curious sight awaited them. Crowding the cart track beyond the gate was a throng of men, women, children, and dogs, obviously curious about the commotion in the cherry orchard. The men chatted together in small groups, decorously pretending to be occupied with one another, but the women were unabashedly inquisitive. Jan could feel their eyes appraise her with sidelong interest as a few called a greeting to her parents. *"Bonjour, m'sieur. Bonjour, madame."* The voices were pleasant enough, but they had a puzzled, questioning inflection.

The Nelsons replied politely but did not tarry. Only Tony seemed to take the scene in stride. He grinned at everyone, shouted a cheery "Hi!" and took off at a run, beating the rest back to the Centre.

Walking abreast, the other three crossed the square slowly. "Word of your legacy seems to have spread, Margot," Mr. Nelson said. "We're causing quite a stir."

"It isn't us. It's the house," Jan observed.

"But the house has been here since the nineteenth century."

"I wish you spoke good French, Doug," said Mrs. Nelson. "I'd give a lot to know what's going on."

So would I, Jan thought, and suddenly wondered if Eric Stockton could help them.

"My French isn't so bad," her father was saying. "I could ask Sister Agatha a few leading questions, but I doubt if she's up to discussing our mysterious appeal." As they entered the gate he changed the subject. "Let's get cleaned up and drive into Avallon for paint, etcetera and let the townspeople stare."

Unexpectedly the Sisters offered the Nelsons lunch—bowls of bean soup and crusty rolls, baked in the Centre's kitchen. They ate at a scrubbed pine table with the nuns. Tony, who was famished, had three helpings. Jan found the hot food a welcome change from picnic fare, but she regretted that there was no chance to talk to Sister Agatha, who sat at the far end of the table and ate quickly, with lowered eyes. Although they were friendly and pleasant to the Americans, within the limitations of the language barrier, the other nuns seemed preoccupied and unapproachable.

Following a detailed map, Mr. Nelson took a circuitous route to Avallon that led through the Vallée du Cousin. "We might as well do a little sightseeing," he said. "The stores won't open until three o'clock."

The valley road was cool and shady, wandering beside a rock-strewn stream and bordered by tree-clad cliffs. Ferns brushed the car wheels, and water dripped from the dark stones. Compared to the sunny fields surounding Vezelay, this area was another world.

Jan, however, was scarcely conscious of the scenery. Her thoughts kept returning to the freakish little house in the cherry orchard. Why had the villagers shunned it before, yet been seemingly drawn to it this morning? What made it both frightening and provocative?

The house had a secret. Of that she was sure. A guilty secret? Riding through the narrow, crowded streets of Avallon, Jan kept trying to imagine what the secret could possibly be.

While her mother bought paint, brushes, rollers, and a can of turpentine, Jan was sent off to find a dustpan and brush. It wasn't easy. All of the stores were small specialty shops. The only big supermarket was one they had passed on the outskirts of town.

Tony had followed his father, and they reappeared hauling a carton as big as a suitcase. "What's in that?" Mrs. Nelson asked, as they lifted it into the rear of the car.

"It's a surprise," said Tony with a delighted grin. "Dad said not to tell."

After a stop at the supermarket for canned goods and staples, Jan rode back to Vezelay wedged among bags and boxes. The family's conversation eddied around her, but she wasn't listening. She was thinking about Eric, wondering whether he could be persuaded to tell her all he knew about the old house.

Glancing over her shoulder from the front seat, Mrs. Nelson said, "You're very quiet, Jan. Feeling all right? We could change places."

"I'm fine, thanks," Jan replied. "Besides, we're almost there."

The conical hill loomed off to the right, beige and gray stone outlined against a clear blue sky. The ascent of the rue St. Étienne no longer seemed perilous. Had it been only yesterday her father had inched the car up in first gear? Today he was driving in third. The *charcuterie,* where a brisk little woman cut and trimmed the meats she sold, was becoming familiar, as were the other stores. The townspeople, however, appeared as enigmatic as ever, and Jan feared they were likely to remain so.

Piling out of the Fiat at their usual parking place, the Nelsons gathered up all the bundles and bags they could carry. The big box with its surprise contents would have to wait for a second trip.

As usual, Tony led the way through the alley. Then, halfway to the orchard gate, he stopped abruptly and turned around. "Say, gang, what's happened to all our junk?" he called.

Jan stared in astonishment at the fence line. Where nearly thirty heavy blue bags had been stationed there was only a long line of crushed weeds.

4

For a few seconds everyone was speechless. Then Mrs. Nelson offered the most logical explanation. "Maybe the trash collector came by."

"Naw." Tony shook his head. "They collect once a week, on Thursdays. This is Friday."

"How do you know so much?" Jan asked.

With a lopsided grin intended as a leer, Tony said, "I get around."

"You sure do," Jan agreed. "You've got a disappearing act you could sell to television."

Pretending to be naive, Tony asked, "You really think so?"

"Come along," said Mrs. Nelson. "These bags are heavy."

"I also know," Tony continued, "that the French call a trash collector an *éboueur*. There's an old fellow lives down the way—he's retired now—who's been the Vezelay trashman ever since he was eighteen years old."

"You're making that up," Jan accused him.

"I am not. Eric told me."

"Who's Eric?" Mrs. Nelson asked.

"Mom! You can't have forgotten the guy who cut this path for us just yesterday."

"Yesterday? It seems like a week ago." Mrs. Nelson laughed at her apparent vagueness. "It was only Eric's name I had forgotten."

"Where did you see Eric, Tony?" Jan asked.

"Down the road. He spends vacations here with his family in a house in the village. This morning he was weeding somebody's vegetable patch. That's what he does during the summer—yard work."

"And winter?" asked his father, as he unlocked the door.

"In winter he lives in Paris and goes to college." Tony looked impish. "Any more questions?"

Jan, along with her parents, fell silent. As she dumped the bags she was carrying on the table the gray walls and dirty floors made her feel depressed. And there were two bedrooms at the back still to be cleaned! "When are you planning on moving in here, Mother?" she asked.

"Tomorrow perhaps," said Mrs. Nelson brightly.

Nobody took her seriously. The notion was so fantastic that her husband didn't even bother to object. Jan was wishing the encounter with Eric had been hers instead of Tony's. There were several questions she wanted to ask him. As for her father, he was still bemused by the fate of the trash. "I thought we'd have to hire someone to cart it away," he said.

"Well, now you don't have to," said Tony.

"Don't be too sure." Jan still felt dejected. "There will be just as many bags again tomorrow."

"Look on the bright side, Jan." Mrs. Nelson patted her arm comfortingly. "One more day and the worst will be over. We might even get the kitchen painted if we all work very hard." She directed her glance at Tony.

"I'm a good painter!"

So far as Jan could recall, Tony had never picked up a paintbrush in his life. She was about to say so when her mother dodged the issue with a compliment. "I don't doubt it, Tony, but we need you men for the heavy work."

Outside there was a crackling of twigs that announced someone approaching. Jan swung around in time to see Eric duck under the arbor. He looked totally dumbfounded.

"I heard voices as I was passing by," he said, when he reached the open door, "and I couldn't believe my ears." His glance swept the room, the shopping bags on the table, and the four faces. Trying to understand the situation, he asked, "What are you *doing* here?"

Mrs. Nelson's laughter made light of his astonishment. "We own the place," she said. "You ran off yesterday before we had a chance to tell you."

"But you're not planning to *live* here?"

"Not permanently," Mrs. Nelson explained. "Just for the rest of the summer."

"Didn't Tony tell you?" asked Jan in surprise.

"I thought you knew," Tony said to Eric. "Everybody else does. You should have seen the crowd around our gate this noon!"

Leaning against the nearest wall as if he needed temporary support, Eric said, "I'll just bet! You must be a sensation."

"I suppose the French can't imagine Americans who'd be willing to live in such a hovel," said Mrs. Nelson with sudden asperity. Her eyes flashed as she defended the right to occupy her own house.

"It's going to be like camp," Tony explained eagerly. "No john even."

"That's not what I'm talking about." Eric spoke slowly, apparently ill at ease.

"Then what are you talking about?" Mr. Nelson inquired briskly.

Unoffended, Eric replied, "Nobody has been willing to live here, and not many people have even set foot in the orchard, ever since. . . ."

Jan wished he would stop talking in riddles. "Since what?"

"Since the murder," he said, then noticed her widening eyes. "Good Lord, didn't you know?"

"Murder?" Jan spoke dully.

"Murder!" exclaimed Tony in excitement.

His father said, "Sh!" as though the word should be whispered, if spoken at all.

"I think you'd better sit down, Eric." Mrs. Nelson indicated the rump-sprung armchair in the corner. "Now tell us who was murdered. When? And why?"

"Oh, it was a long time ago, back in the forties, after the war," Eric said, as though trying to diminish the crime by placing it far in the past. "Before I was born, of course, so all I have is hearsay."

"We understand," said Mr. Nelson, nodding.

"Both brothers were living here then, I believe. Armand Frechette—the one who died last year—was the younger. Jacques, the older one, had been injured in the war. I'm not quite sure how. A grenade or something. Anyway, he wasn't quite right in the head afterward, according to village gossip, and he kept talking about having a fortune hidden somewhere in this house. That's why he was killed, people think, but nobody knows what the fortune was or if it was ever discovered."

Tony was too enthralled to interrupt, but Mr. Nelson asked, "Who was the murderer?"

"Nobody knows that either. The police never found out."

Tony gave a long-drawn-out whistle.

"My father says it was a pretty grisly affair," Eric continued. "The news made all the Paris papers, of course, and Vezelay was suddenly famous. For a while, I'm told, this house was a bigger attraction than the basilica."

Jan shivered.

"Now only elderly visitors remember that a crime was committed here, but in the village there isn't a child over ten who hasn't heard the story, and not a man or woman who doesn't have a personal theory about the case."

Mrs. Nelson sighed. "Well, that explains a lot."

It certainly does, Jan was thinking. The reaction of the Franciscan Sisters, the crowd at the gate this noon, the remark made by the clerk at the tourist bureau. She glanced at her father, who seemed lost in thought. "Do you suppose—" she started, then stopped short.

Eric looked her way. "Suppose what?"

Instead of meeting his eyes, Jan turned to her parents. "I was wondering about the trash bags," she confessed.

"So was I," said her father, and he recounted the incident for Eric's benefit. "When we got back from

Avallon," he concluded, "every last bag had disappeared."

Eric burst out laughing, as if this turn of events was a marvelous joke. "Can't you guess what happened to them?" he asked. "The villagers simply waited until you were gone, then carted them off."

"But why?" Jan asked. "Why would anyone want all those rotting, filthy clothes and all the other junk?"

"Remember the prizes at the bottom of cereal boxes?"

"There were no prizes in those bags!" Mrs. Nelson wrinkled her nose in distaste.

"Probably not, but there's always a chance, and the villagers want to make sure. I bet they'll paw through every inch of that rubbish and open the seams of all the old coats and suits, even if they have to wear clothespins on their noses."

"Looking for what?" asked Mr. Nelson.

Eric shrugged. "The mysterious treasure." He added quickly, "If it still exists."

"Money, you mean?" Tony bounced out of his chair in chagrin. "There could be folding money sewn into those clothes?" His eyes grew round with concern. "Hey, maybe we've thrown away a fortune!"

Shaking his head, Eric said, "I doubt if you've thrown away even a ten-franc note."

Tony looked relieved. "Then what—"

"I was thinking about something quite different," said Eric. He gestured toward the road. "Do you know the name of that street that leads downhill? It's called the rue de l'Argentière."

"*Argent*. I get it," said Tony.

"Back in the Middle Ages there was a mint in one of those old buildings."

"Vezelay struck its own coins?" Mr. Nelson sounded surprised and interested.

"So I'm told. My parents know a lot more about Vezelay history than I do. You'll have to meet them."

"We'd enjoy that," said Mr. Nelson. "But to go back to the mint. I suppose if a number of those early coins turned up, they'd be worth a great deal to collectors."

Eric nodded. "I've never even seen one. They're very rare."

"Maybe the villagers aren't so stupid," said Tony, trying to sound grown-up.

"They're not stupid at all, Tony. Many of them are quite shrewd."

"But somebody ransacked the house years and years ago," Jan reminded him. "Then why go through the trash bags?"

"Because the search was probably hasty and no treasure of any sort was found." Eric glanced back at Tony. "Nor was the murderer."

While Tony thought that remark over, Eric

turned back to Mr. Nelson. "The coin theory is only one of half a dozen or more that the villagers have about the fortune that could have been hidden here. Nobody knows for sure there was one. The murder could have been an act of vengeance, or it could have been the result of a quarrel and have nothing at all to do with greed."

Mrs. Nelson, who had been listening quietly, leaned toward Eric. "Was Armand Frechette ever suspected?" she asked.

"I haven't any idea. If it matters to you, maybe my father would know." He stood up and said with an apologetic grin, "Here I am, getting to Alexandra's late again. I go to her place last thing in the afternoon."

Who Alexandra was the Nelsons did not immediately discover. Eric took off at a dogtrot, leaving them a great deal to think about. Then, suddenly, he reappeared. "I don't work on Saturdays," he said, "so I'll stop by in the morning to see if I can be of any help."

"Well," said Mrs. Nelson after a few minutes, "my head is spinning, but I suppose my arms and legs will still behave normally. Shall we put in another hour's work?"

Instead of protesting, Tony was enthusiastic. "Hey, Mom, I'll help load bags. Finders keepers, OK?"

"It is not OK at all," said his father sharply. "Everything in this house belongs to your mother. Remember that!"

"It belongs to all of us, darling," said Mrs. Nelson, "but don't get your hopes up, Tony. I'm afraid the debris we're bagging is just what we thought it was —junk."

5

A murder in this very cottage!

Jan was so shaken by the news that she forgot the big box containing her father's present, still locked in the car.

So did the rest of the family. Not until bedtime did Jan hear Tony ask, "Say, Dad, what about the surprise?"

With a snap of his fingers, Mr. Nelson acknowledged that he too had forgotten the gift. "It can wait for morning," he said, yawning. "Christmas in July."

"Better than Christmas!" cried Mrs. Nelson, when the box was carted to the cottage the next morning. She lifted a two-burner electric stove from its cardboard coverings, then flung her arms around her husband's neck and hugged him ecstatically. "Hot water!"

"And hot food, I hope."

"Soup for lunch, if we can find a can opener!"

Tony elected to stay inside and paw through every piece of trash in the bedrooms before he stuffed it into bags. "I'm looking for some of that treasure Eric was talking about," he admitted.

"You're looking for a needle in a haystack," his mother said, but she left him to his search, which was a form of play. Together she and Jan were starting to paint the kitchen, and there was a conquering light in her eyes.

The ceiling was low, the room small. White paint made a quick and remarkable transformation. Jan stood off and acknowledged to herself a growing belief that the place could be made livable.

Working on opposite walls, the two chatted together companionably. "I have a sketchbook and some grease crayons in my suitcase," Jan said. "Once the undergrowth is cut down, there should be a great view over the valley here."

Her mother agreed. "Without a house in sight, except that old shepherd's hut on the opposite hillside."

"I'm not much good at landscapes," Jan mused. "Maybe I should start with a street scene."

"There are some nice old houses on the rue St.

Étienne," said her mother. "There's one with a window box filled with red geraniums that looks very paintable."

"And we haven't even started to explore!" This morning Jan wanted to talk about anything but the murder, yet all sorts of questions kept nagging her. Where, in what room, had her great-uncle Jacques been murdered? And, more importantly, why?

Outside, her father was greeting Eric, who had brought along a saw and another pair of big clippers. Tony rushed to the door to call a cheerful hello, but quickly returned to his treasure seeking. Glancing into the bedroom where he was working, Jan could see that bags were being stuffed at a very slow pace indeed.

Having worked his way around the house clockwise, Mr. Nelson was about to attack the bushes along the one remaining wall, which carried the flue of the kitchen stove through an aperture in the thick stone. It was the side where Tony had heard the disturbing noises on the night of their arrival.

"I suppose there's an attic above these rooms," Jan could hear her father saying, as she rolled on another strip of paint, "but there doesn't seem to be any way to get up to it. No trapdoor inside, anyway."

"Sometimes there are outside stairs on these old houses," Eric said.

"Wouldn't that be great? Tony could sleep in the attic." Jan spoke hopefully.

The word *attic* must have carried to the next room, because Tony stopped digging for treasure and dashed out the back door, as eager as a Spanish conquistador seeking a new country to conquer.

"Maybe that's where they kept the loot!" he was shouting at the top of his lungs.

Jan cringed, but her mother laughed. "He'll grow up," she said. "You did."

Jan chuckled. "Maybe I tried harder."

As she spoke Eric's voice carried through the open kitchen window. "Look, Mr. Nelson, we're in luck. No stairs, but there's a ladder."

"A new ladder!" Tony cried.

A new ladder? Jan and her mother exchanged glances, then put down their paint rollers and went outside. Leaning against the side of the house was a tall, unpainted wooden ladder, obviously new.

Glancing up the steep slope toward the road, invisible beyond the vine-entangled trees, Jan could make out the scars left by the ladder when it had been dragged through the orchard to the house. She turned to look up and saw that a big door in the wooden siding under the eaves had been shoved open. Jan gasped in surprise, astounded that they hadn't noticed it before. The undergrowth on this side of the house was so dense, however, that no one had been tempted to explore the section.

Already Tony was on the fourth rung of the ladder, climbing fast. "Wow!" he muttered.

Seconds later he reached the top and peered inside. "Hey, you guys," he called down in excitement. "Whaddaya know? Somebody's been stamping around up here." He disappeared from sight, then shouted again, "Wow, does he have *beeg* feet! You should see his footprints."

"Stay away from those footprints," his father called back, as he started to climb the ladder.

"Why?" Tony asked, coming to the door and looking down. "Oh, I getcha. Cops and robbers!"

"Just do as I say." His father spoke impatiently, then turned and beckoned. "Margot, you'd better come up."

Equally curious, Jan followed, with Eric coming on her heels. Moving cautiously on the dusty floor, they all stood looking down at the footprints, two of which were remarkably distinct. They had been made by a man's heavy boots, which were very large indeed.

"See," said Tony, "I told you, Dad. That was no animal! These footprints are still fresh." He turned to Eric. "We heard him ourselves, prowling around, night before last."

Jan bent to examine the footprints more closely. The soles of the boots were corrugated like a rubber tire, making furrows that formed a pattern in the dust. She wished she had her crayons here, so that she could make an outline of one of the prints. How could she manage to protect it for a while!

As she pondered, Mrs. Nelson spoke. "How very peculiar! Do you realize, Doug, that nothing has been disturbed up here? Although the rest of the house has been ransacked, the attic hasn't been touched. I wonder why?"

Eric turned away from the rest. "From the outside," he said perceptively, "unless somebody looked closely or was acquainted with the house from the old days, he wouldn't be apt to discover an entrance. I'll bet the door looks like part of the wall when it's shut."

Mr. Nelson agreed. "Nevertheless, we've had an intruder bent on mischief. What do we do about it? Tell the *gendarmes*?"

Eric looked thoughtful. "I suppose so, but you'll be stirring up a hornet's nest. The house has always been a village curiosity, and the knowledge that somebody has broken in can mean only one thing."

"Which is?"

"That there's something worth stealing still left in the house."

"Or that the thief *thinks* there is," Mrs. Nelson appended.

"For the moment," said Mr. Nelson, considering, "let's keep the police out of it. The incident is over and done with, and we're hoping to settle down to a quiet summer." With a wry quirk of his mouth, he added, "Eventually."

Jan was looking around. From what she could see

of the attic's contents, they had little chance of finding treasure here, among discards of a bygone age. There was a dismantled brass bedstead with a mattress and springs leaning against it, three elderly trunks with bonnet tops, a shaving stand, a footstool with three legs, a row of boxes tied with cord, and a four-drawer bureau of dark wood. The door was the only opening.

Yet Tony asked eagerly, "When can I start to sleep up here?"

"There's no window," Jan reminded him.

"I can leave the door open."

Jan shuddered. "Suppose that man comes back?"

"We can move the ladder away." Not easily frightened, Tony had an answer to everything.

Walking gingerly on the dusty floor, Jan moved across the room toward a cardboard carton. She took out several empty jelly glasses, shook out a few dead bugs, and turned the box upside down over the clearer of the two distinguishable footprints. "Don't touch this, anybody," she said, looking at Tony.

"Why not?"

"I want to make a crayon outline of the footprint, just for fun."

"It's not for fun, and you know it. You're playing Nancy Drew," Tony teased.

Flushing, Jan bit off a reply, then glanced at Eric, but he was paying no heed to the interchange. Fingering one of the jelly glasses, he was saying to Mrs.

Nelson, "These are the fine old ones. Feel. They have single instead of double rims. My mother collects them for drinking glasses. They're really neat."

A few minutes later Mrs. Nelson made a find of her own—a drawer full of linens, yellowed with age but intact. There were a dozen real linen dish towels that had never been used, along with bed sheets and square pillow slips of coarse cotton. In the remaining bureau drawers, down comforters were stuffed. "Christmas again!" She spoke delightedly.

Forming a line on the ladder, everyone passed the booty from hand to hand. Then Eric helped Mr. Nelson drag the mattresses from the bedrooms to the sunny side of the house. There they leaned them against the wall and swept them off. Jan and her mother went back to the kitchen again and started to paint as fast as possible, to make up for lost time.

By noon, when Eric left for home, they had only one wall left to finish, so they sent Tony for a *baguette* and went on working. While he was gone Mr. Nelson unearthed a can opener from the "saved" items and put soup to heating on the new stove.

Midafternoon saw the kitchen walls covered with a first coat of paint, the floor scrubbed, and the bedrooms swept out. Ten more bags full of trash were leaning against the fence up by the road, but the sounds of activity coming from the cottage apparently discouraged anyone from carting them off.

"Do you think we can stay here tonight, Doug?"

As Jan knew, all along this move had been her mother's aim.

"If you're game, Margot, I am."

"Mission accomplished," Jan murmured, as her father spoke.

Everyone went back to the Centre, where they showered and changed into clean clothes. Late in the afternoon they said good-bye to the nuns and carried their luggage down to the cottage. Tony agreed to sleep on quilts spread on the kitchen floor. "But only temporarily!" Jan was given the smaller of the two bedrooms.

"Until I can rig up an outside shower," her father observed, "I guess we'll have to take our baths in the river."

A few minutes later a boy who looked close to Tony's age arrived at the door. He smiled shyly and handed Mrs. Nelson an unsealed envelope.

She read the enclosed note quickly. "Eric's parents would like us to come by for an hour after dinner." Glancing from face to face, she saw that she could safely add, "Tell them we'll be delighted." Then, with a friendly smile, she said, "You must be Eric's brother."

Irrepressible, Tony stepped forward and said, "I'm Tony. What's your name?"

"My name is Joel." The boy nodded his head in a gesture that was almost a bow and extended his hand.

Tony stared at the hand in confusion, so his mother stepped into the breach, shook Joel's hand, and introduced him to the others. After the boy had left, she rumpled Tony's hair affectionately, shaking her head in amusement mingled with maternal despair. "You'll have to learn French maners."

"Joel's not French. He's American," Tony protested.

"He must have been raised in France, dear. He speaks English with a French accent. I suspect he's lived here most of his life."

And so it proved. Joel had lived in Paris since early childhood, while Eric had gone to elementary school in the United States. Like their children, the Stocktons were bilingual. To Jan, they seemed more French than American.

Mr. Stockton was a thin man with a shaggy red beard and piercing blue eyes, which regarded her from behind horn-rimmed glasses. He and Joel were very much of a type, but Eric looked more like his mother, whose long, soft hair tumbled from the pins with which she tried to anchor it on top of her head. Like Eric's, her eyes were the soft, tawny color of amber, matching the smock she wore over paint-stained jeans.

Hospitably, the Stocktons served wine and soft drinks. They seemed pleased that the house in the cherry orchard would be occupied for the summer.

"Before the wilderness took over, I used to go up there to paint," Mrs. Stockton said.

Jan was fascinated by the paintings on the walls, unframed canvases that were fresh and colorful. She left the group and roamed about, standing before each in turn.

After a short time, Mrs. Stockton joined her. "You're interested in painting?" she asked.

Jan nodded. "I get to the Philadelphia Museum once in a while. And I sketch a little," she added diffidently, "just for fun."

"Lovely. What a time you'll have here!"

Jan couldn't leave the paintings. "You did these?"

Mrs. Stockton nodded.

"I don't entirely understand them," Jan confessed, "but I like them a lot."

The others were moving out to a walled terrace at the rear of the tall, narrow house, which was situated halfway down the hill. "We've been coming here for six years now," Mr. Stockton was saying. "In the winter I teach in Paris. Vezelay is our summer escape hatch. We love the place."

"And we hope you will, too," said Mrs. Stockton to the Nelsons, as she came out to the terrace with Jan. "Don't let village gossip disturb you. Your cottage has a superb location, and I'm sure you'll be perfectly safe."

"Mother means you should forget the murder

bit," said Eric ruefully. "She wishes I hadn't been the one to tell you. So do I." He spoke to Mrs. Nelson, not to Jan.

Bursting to wedge a few words into the conversation, Tony forestalled any reply. "My dad's a teacher too," he told Mr. Stockton proudly.

"In secondary school," said Mr. Nelson, faintly disparagingly. "Do you teach at the Sorbonne?" He had always regretted his lack of a doctorate, because he would have enjoyed teaching at college level.

Mr. Stockton nodded. "My field is anthropology. And yours?"

"I teach history." Mr. Nelson replied.

"You should see the Roman ruins near St. Père," Mr. Stockton said. "It's only a few miles from here."

As the men went on talking, Jan's mother turned to her hostess. "Actually," she admitted, "the murder mystery adds a little fillip to my legacy. Besides, it all happened such a long time ago that the house is quite free of ghosts." She added as an afterthought, "You know, I never met my Uncle Armand, who left me the property."

"Neither did we, of course," said Mrs. Stockton. "There are people in the village who remember him, though. Older folk, in their seventies."

"The mayor, for one," said Mr. Stockton, rejoining the general conversation.

"And the former trash collector," added Eric.

"What about the caretaker at the basilica?" asked his mother. "He's old enough."

"He might not have lived here back in the forties, but I could ask." Again Eric spoke directly to Mrs. Nelson, as if he wanted to please her. When she didn't reply, he stepped away from the group and turned toward the view.

Hoping to get better acquainted, Jan moved over to stand beside him, but a conversational opening was hard to find. Eric was no help. Suddenly he seemed glum and self-absorbed.

Still, Jan made a polite effort. "Tony and Joel seem to have struck up a friendship," she said, as the two boys went inside.

"Yes."

"Dad really appreciated your help today."

"No trouble."

He's a curious sort, Jan thought, pricked by annoyance. Why can't he treat me as pleasantly as he treats my mother? Although she needed a friend almost as much as her brother, she didn't intend to chase this young man. Two people could play at being taciturn. Abruptly she turned away and went back to the others.

Her parents were consulting the Stocktons about possible motives for the murder. "Do you think there's a chance that my Uncle Jacques was fooling everyone, that he was quite mad?" Jan's mother asked.

"It's a possibility," Mr. Stockton replied, "but I've always clung to the notion that Jacques Frechette had hidden something of real value, something worth killing for."

Privately Jan thought that Eric's father assumed too much in using the past tense. Something of value might still be hidden in the house. The hope was faint but real.

"Everybody has a pet theory on what it might have been," said Mrs. Stockton, still using the past tense. "Eric included."

Mr. Stockton smiled. "Yes. He likes the idea of a cache of coins from the medieval mint, but it's equally possible that Jacques found and hid an especially rare and interesting fossil. The fields are full of bits and pieces, you know."

Overhearing, Joel came out of the house carrying a large rock in which half a chambered nautilus was fossilized.

"Sometimes I follow the farmers when they do their plowing," he explained, seeming considerably less shy on his home ground than he had when appearing at the cottage. "Look at this. If it was perfect, it might be a museum piece."

"Or you could sell it," suggested Tony, his eye on the main chance.

"You're not supposed to, if it's really valuable,"

Joel told him. "But some people do, don't they, Pop?"

"Although it's against the law, I'm afraid so. There are always rich people with very few scruples about how they build their collections."

Tony was charmed by the notion of looking for fossils. "Can you show me how?" he asked Joel, as if doing so were some new kind of game. Pleased by an affirmative answer, he kept on asking questions, one after another, as he followed Joel back into the house. Jan gazed after the two boys rather wistfully, wishing that she too could find a companion of her own age.

Did Eric consider her too young to be interesting? she wondered. He was in college while she was still in high school. She guessed his age at about nineteen. Sitting on the low wall that surrounded the terrace on three sides, he looked morose and lonely. Perhaps, like Joel, he was basically rather shy.

Approaching him again, tentatively, Jan was surprised when he suddenly raised his head and looked up at the sky. "Here they come!" he cried.

High above the low hills that ringed the valley rode three huge balloons. Enormous flowers, painted in the French tricolors, decorated their inflated sides. Too far away to seem real, they were a spectacular sight. The wicker gondolas looked smaller than orioles' nests from where Jan stood, and the balloonists themselves were invisible.

Not only were the giant bubbles dramatic. The twilit ambiance in which they drifted, the cool evening air, and the spreading Burgundian fields had a theatrical, almost dreamlike quality. "Aren't they marvelous!" Jan murmured appreciatively.

"Have you ever been up?" Eric asked.

"In a balloon?" Jan shook her head. The possibility had never even occurred to her.

"I'm hoping to go, if a space opens up, before the end of the summer." Eric spoke softly, as though he was divulging a secret.

"A space?"

Eric nodded. "The balloons are booked for months—sometimes years—in advance. My only chance will be if somebody gets sick or breaks a leg or something." He grinned roguishly. "Not that I wish them any hard luck."

Wanting to keep the conversation going, Jan asked, "Does it cost a lot? For a single ride, I mean?"

"It costs plenty. I'm saving money as fast as I can."

Still keeping her eyes on the balloons, Jan said, "It must be entirely different from flying in a plane. Out in the open. Just floating in the sky. No noise."

Refuting this conception, one of the balloons made a hissing sound, and Eric laughed. "Just letting off a little hot air."

"I wonder where they'll come down?"

"It depends partly on the breeze and partly on the

pilot's decision. He always tries to pick a good landing spot."

The balloons drifted over the basilica and disappeared from sight, and after another half hour Jan walked back home with Tony and her parents. She felt happy and refreshed. Eric was not a lost cause.

6

"Alexandra's."

The place where Eric worked in the late afternoons intrigued Jan. Who was Alexandra—girl or woman? Why was it important to be on time?

Eric regularly wheeled his bicycle up past the cherry orchard, so Jan assumed that he was heading toward the only private house situated above the cottage on the hill, the big place that abutted the cathedral square. The house had an archway curving over the cobbled alley to a wall opposite. Every time Jan went on an errand to the village she walked under it, passing the door in the wall that Tony had found locked.

Undoubtedly, he had tried the door a second time, and probably a third. Tony was a curious boy, and Jan was not without curiosity herself.

Yet, newly aware of the value the French placed on privacy, she was sure that the door was locked against prying tourists roaming the precincts of the Madeleine and did not want to test it.

There were plenty of new tourists each day. They swarmed through the gift shops and the parking lots, went on hour-long tours of the basilica, and came out with cricks in their necks from looking up at the Romanesque sculptures on top of the tall columns.

Some sought the stone benches in the square, but others roamed the narrow streets, peering into private alleys and gardens. There were Germans and Dutch, Spanish, Japanese, French, Americans. Most were soft-spoken and polite, but a few were noisy and downright snoopy. These people, as she acquired the point of view of a local resident, Jan began to despise.

Carrying a string bag filled with groceries, she was on her way home on Monday afternoon when the town clock chimed five musical notes. Under the archway two young men, wearing dirty shorts and carrying motorcycle helmets, were taking alternate swigs from a bottle. One was leaning against the door in the wall when it suddenly gave way and he fell backward. The bottle flew out of his hand as he landed on a stone platform and sprayed its contents on the freshly mowed grass below.

Jan, who had been about to pass, stopped spellbound. She was looking down at a stretch of grass like green velvet, bordered with flower beds so bright and sumptuous that they looked almost unreal. On her knees at the end of the lawn was a woman with carrot-colored hair. She was wearing jeans and had a trowel in her hand, but from the distance at which she stood Jan couldn't tell whether she was more likely to be Eric's assistant or the lady of the house.

Eric himself was approaching the open door at a run. He came up a flight of stone steps two at a time and spoke solicitously. "I hope you didn't hurt yourself."

The motorcyclist, on his feet now, was rubbing his back. "So if I did it would be your fault, for leaving that door there unlocked!"

Privately relieved that the fellow spoke English with a Cockney accent and therefore couldn't be tagged as American, Jan started to walk on when Eric spotted her. "Wait a minute! Come on inside," he called. At the same time he was moving forward, keeping his temper but unmistakably urging the young man back to the street.

Jan slipped past the pair and waited on the high platform, which was flanked by two pairs of stone steps set into the wall. With a sigh of relief, Eric closed the door and slid the bolt. "I usually remember to lock it," he said, then gave a slight shrug. "No matter. Come meet Alexandra. She's been asking about you folks."

The woman kneeling on the ground rocked back on her heels and stood up as Jan and Eric approached. She took off a garden glove and held out her hand. "Good afternoon," she said with a slight foreign accent. "My name is Alexandra Jourdan. I hear we're going to be neighbors."

The hand Jan held briefly was slender but strong, the grasp as powerful as a man's. "I'm Janice Nelson," she said. Then she added, "Yes, we're going to spend the summer here."

As she spoke she was wondering why the owner of this spacious and elegant garden had the French name of Jourdan when she didn't look French. She had a lithe body, a long thin neck, and a face crisscrossed by a multitude of fine lines. Above the aging face the red hair looked utterly incongruous but oddly becoming.

"Eric has been telling me about the wretched condition in which you found the cottage." Alexandra's voice was low and sympathetic. "What a disappointment, when you have come so far!"

Jan nodded. "It's still in a mess, but we're working on it." Standing with the heavy string bag dangling from her hand, Jan suddenly felt unequal to the situation. She turned away from Alexandra's inquiring black eyes and from the view of the great house rising beyond the wall and said, "My, what a marvelous garden!"

"You like it?" Alexandra seemed pleased. "I spend most afternoons out here. It is my one hobby."

The flawlessness of the mulched flower beds, the clipped yews, the sweep of grass as smooth as a golf-course green were in such contrast to the state of the cherry orchard that Jan burst into laughter and suddenly relaxed. "I can't believe this! Our place is a jungle."

"Ah, but you have a father and a brother to clean it up. And I understand Eric also has been helping. She put a hand lightly on Eric's tanned arm. "He is a good helper, although he doesn't know a rose from a poppy." She spoke in a whisper and grinned wickedly.

Eric smiled down at Alexandra so warmly that Jan was quite surprised. "I'm not making gardening my career," he reminded her.

The exchange apparently amused Mrs. Jourdan. She stripped off her second glove, revealing a ring set with a huge emerald surrounded by diamonds. "Come on," she cried. "Enough for today. Let's go inside and have a glass of tea." She beamed at Jan, who became aware that Alexandra's face, although wrinkled as a walnut, had charm and character. "I like young people. Besides, when my husband is in Paris, I become hungry for companionship."

At the top of the garden steps, a walkway led across the arch to French doors opening into a big living room. Pausing on the threshold, Jan noticed that, except for great bowls of fresh flowers, everything in the room was pale gray-blue—woodwork, walls, cabinets, and the damask coverings of delicate antique furniture. Nothing distracted from the effect of the brilliant blooms, not even the paintings on the walls, which were soft-colored and impressionistic. There was taste and quality here, as well as great luxury.

Jan put her bag of groceries on the floor beside the doors. "May I help?" she asked, as Alexandra crossed the floor.

"Thank you, but I'd prefer you to stay here and entertain Eric." Her eyes twinkled as Eric flushed.

Instead of trying to start a conversation with Eric, Jan wandered around the room, stopping here and there in front of a curio cabinet. "The Jourdans must be very rich," she said to break the rather strained silence.

"Yes."

"This is a lovely room—so serene."

"You should see their house in Paris," Eric said, responding at last. "It's in a marvelous part of the city, overlooking the Ile St. Louis."

"Is it as large as this?"

"Three times as large. It's simply fabulous, filled with Lionel's remarkable things."

"You've been there then?" Jan asked, a trifle surprised.

Eric nodded. "The Jourdans are friends of my parents. Dad helped Lionel put together a collection of Javanese puppets. Usually, however, he buys only things that are very rare, one of a kind."

"What kind of things?" Jan was intrigued. She had never known a collector of anything except American antiques.

"Look around. Books, paintings, coins, Vezelay artifacts, almost anything you can think of."

"Vezelay artifacts?"

Eric nodded. "Look at this. He picked up an object from a side table and held it out. "Can you guess what it is?"

Jan took a heavy metal disk in her fingers, examining the engraving on the flat, circular bottom. She shook her head. "I haven't a clue."

"Look at the engraving more closely, Jan. It's a stamp from the Vezelay mint, which means it could be nearly a thousand years old."

Jan was impressed. "Put it back on the table," she told Eric. "I feel shaky about even handling it."

"Fortunately, it won't break," Eric told her. "It's not like Alexandra's icons, some of which are painted on glass."

"Is Mrs. Jourdan Russian?" Jan asked.

"Yes. Didn't you guess? The offer of a glass of tea was the giveaway. Besides, no Frenchwoman would casually invite a stranger into her home."

Alexandra, returning at that moment, overheard the last remark. "Ah, but Russians are different. We must be surrounded by people to feel alive."

Eric crossed the room quickly to take a heavy silver tray from her hands. He set it on a low table without asking where to put it. Alexandra smiled and thanked him in French.

Then, as she poured hot tea into glasses, she turned to Jan. "You see, in St. Petersburg the house was always full of family and relatives. I remember it clearly, although of course I was only a child when we left." Switching to the duties of a hostess, she asked, "Do you take sugar, Janice?"

"One lump, please, Mrs.—or do I call you Madame Jourdan?"

"You call me Alexandra, in order to make an elderly woman feel younger than she should."

Jan said, "Thank you," warmed by the vitality of the little lady, who must be as old as her grandmother, but whose first name seemed quite natural to use.

Alexandra passed a plate of store cookies. "We do not stand on ceremony here, where we keep no help," she said, then started to gossip companionably with Eric about village affairs.

"Of course, you and your family are the most discussed subjects of the moment," she told Jan after a while. "Even the balloonists, who usually get top billing, have had to wait in the wings."

In spite of her Russian accent, Alexandra spoke such easy, colloquial English that Jan was surprised. "In the wings?"

Alexandra nodded. "You're on stage, my dear, until it's decided whether you'll stick it out for the summer or give up and go home."

Jan smiled. "We'll stick it out. You don't know my mother!"

"I'd like to. You must bring her to call someday soon." Refilling the glasses with tea, Alexandra added, "I'm always at home in the late afternoon, after I come in from the garden."

"Mother would adore your garden!" Jan said.

"Then come early. Just knock on the door in the wall."

Jan was relieved that her hostess hadn't suggested coming down to the cottage. From a palace to a place with a backyard privy would be quite a jump.

She said as much to Eric after they left the house.

"You don't understand," Eric said. "The condition of the cottage wouldn't faze Alexandra. In a village of 301 souls, now increased temporarily by the four of you, everyone knows everyone else. Alexandra knows the trash collector, the trash collector is a lifelong friend of the mayor, the priests know not only their parishioners but the renegades of other faiths. As for the Franciscan Sisters, they even know the names of the cats and dogs."

Jan laughed. "That's the longest speech I've ever heard you make," she teased, as she turned toward home.

"Just get me on a subject that interests me," Eric called after her, "and I can talk for hours."

Maybe that was the key to Eric's personality, Jan thought, as she hurried along. Today he had seemed at ease and perfectly natural, as if Alexandra's presence had freed his inhibitions.

A sound from the orchard reached Jan's ears before she emerged from the alley, the grating of a saw on wood. The farmer recommended by Sister Agatha was pruning trees at a steady pace, and it was possible, at last, to see the house from the road.

The man's name, Jan soon learned, was Junot. He was far from young and totally bald, but his gnarled hands were strong, his judgment sure. He worked right along until dusk and said he would be back the next day to cart off the wood.

At least, this schedule was the understanding of Mr. Nelson. The two men conducted a conversation partly in French and partly in sign language, with many nods of the head and appreciative grins, each pleased with the other's efforts.

The last tree to be pruned grew close to the cottage, its branches almost brushing the attic door, which the farmer examined with interest. Beckoning to his employer, he pointed to some deep gashes in the wooden siding, and his rapid French became a virtual torrent.

"What was he saying?" Jan asked her father, when Junot had left.

"I think he was telling me a crowbar was used to open the door and that most people don't know the attic exists, but he uses a patois that bears little relation to my sketchy college French."

Jan discounted her father's modesty, because every day his French was improving. Tony was almost as quick. Starting with no French at all, he began with a few ordinary phrases, most of them questions. *"Qu'est-ce que?"* rose to his lips repeatedly. Meanwhile, Jan and her mother stumbled along with "kitchen" French. They could ask for fruit, cheeses, vegetables, and a few cuts of meat by name, but they acquired no verbs whatsoever.

Immediately after the trees were pruned Tony began a campaign. He was tired of sleeping on the floor and wanted to move up to the attic, which he claimed would be like living in his tree house at home.

To his surprise, his father balked. "When I'm sure it's safe you may, but not until then."

"Safe? I'll be sleeping right over your heads. If I'm scared or anything, I'll pound on the floor and you can come running."

Mr. Nelson shook his head. "Tony, listen to me, and think! Take another look at the size of that footprint Jan outlined with crayon. Also, remember what the farmer said."

"Sure. You told me." Tony looked far from defeated. "So if most people don't know there's an attic here, why wouldn't that make it even safer?"

His father sighed. "I told you to *think*. By now, the way gossip spreads in Vezelay, everybody knows about the attic and may suspect it wasn't ransacked like the rest of the house."

"You mean thieves might come hunting for treasure."

"They might, indeed."

Jan, who was listening, said, "Then we should really get busy and clean the place out."

"We should," said her father. "Tony, you can start tomorrow morning."

"Clean, clean, clean," Tony groaned. "This is where I came in."

"When you're finished, we'll find a lock for the door and cut a window through, so you'll have some light and air," his father promised. He indicated a square no larger than a telephone book with his hands, and Jan knew he was thinking of the tiny panes of red or green glass set high in the walls of Burgundy houses. Scarcely big enough for a squirrel to enter, some were attic windows left open for ventilation. Tony would do quite well with this peephole on the world and a flashlight beside his bed. Not being timorous herself, Jan almost envied him.

Clouds had been building up all evening, not the white puffballs of the past few days, but angry storm clouds that shrouded the tower of the basilica. By morning a steady rain had started, promising to last all day, and at breakfast Jan said to Tony, "I'll help you in the attic, if you like." She was tired of painting and wanted an alternative.

Fortunately, the rain was coming from the north side, so they could leave the big door open wide and get plenty of light as they swept out the loose dust of three decades. Then Jan helped Tony drag the brass bed from under the eaves. The springs were rusty but intact. The mattress, however, was decidedly musty. Jan sniffed and wrinkled her nose, deciding she preferred the downstairs bedroom after all.

Tony, less finicky, bounced on the mattress happily while clouds of foul-smelling dust engulfed him. "Stop!" Jan shouted. "Or I'll leave you to finish this alone."

Since the finders-keepers ploy had been squashed by his father, this prospect was not appealing. Tony calmed down and helped Jan clear out a corner where they could put anything that seemed worth saving. There seemed to be precious little—dingy old-fashioned clothes, broken dishes and bottles, the rubble of lives unknown to Jan.

Although many people had told her that nothing

in Vezelay remained a secret for long, there was one secret nobody had discovered, the motive for the murder of a war-damaged old soldier who lived on the verge of poverty in this simple four-room cottage. What sort of a man, she wondered, could her mother's Uncle Jacques have been?

The attic had not yet provided a clue, although by noon Jan had come across quite a few finds. There was a box of leatherbound books, another carton of jelly glasses, and a trunk containing blankets that must once have been packed away in mothballs, for a faint whiff of the familiar odor drifted through the yellowed newspapers with which they were covered.

"*Paris Soir,*" Jan read, "21 *Janvier*, 1948." Just a few days after the murder! She removed the paper carefully and warned Tony not to touch it.

"Why not?" he asked immediately.

"Because I want to take a look at it, some other time."

"You can't read French."

"No, but Eric can."

"Eric!" Tony scoffed. "You can't get Eric off your mind."

"Tony, that's not true." Although she seethed at the accusation, Jan tried to speak calmly.

"What about yesterday? Chasing him, that's what you were doing."

"You're just jealous," Jan countered, risking her dignity, "because I got invited into Alexandra's garden, when you've been hoping to find the door unlocked."

"Oh, knock it off," grumbled Tony, and Jan knew she had hit on the truth. Her brother stopped teasing her about Eric and went back to work.

A cardboard box filled with old snapshots and postcards was their next find. At the bottom was a stack of photographs. "Gosh, are these guys weird!" Tony commented. "Take a look at the haircuts. Not to mention the clothes! I'm glad I didn't live in olden times."

Jan put the box aside, saying, "Mother may want to go through it." Maybe they had found the answer to Jacques Frechette's appearance, if not the clue to his personality.

A few minutes later Tony blew the dust off the top of a packet of old letters, then picked them up by a rotting string. "What about these?"

"Put them in the same box," Jan suggested. She had carried a pair of school copybooks to the door and opened them to marvel at the fine, slanting penmanship. Compared to Tony's misspelled scribbling, it was remarkable, more like the calligraphy of monks than the careful work of childish hands.

Jan saved the copybooks too and put them on top of the bureau along with an old family Bible, the leather cover of which hung by only a thread or two. Tony at once swept them off, saying, "Hey, that's my bureau!" and carried them over to an empty trunk.

In an effort at organization, Jan put the letters and the box of snapshots and postcards in beside them, then shut the lid. Noticing a key in the lock, she tried it and found that it worked. On an impulse she put the key in her pocket. At least no burglar could walk off with these things before her mother had a chance to go through them, she thought to herself.

"I'm getting hungry, aren't you?" Tony spoke from a far corner, where he was tugging at a box too heavy to handle alone.

"Come to think of it, I am," Jan said, "but let's wait till we're called." She helped push the box to the center of the room and gazed proudly at the half dozen filled trash bags.

Cutting the cord with his pocket knife, Tony opened the box and peered inside. "Nothing but a bunch of rocks," he said in disappointment.

Then an idea struck him. "Say, though, they may be fossils!" Settling down on the floor Indian-fashion, he picked up one after another. After examining several in turn, he put them back in the box. "They sure don't look like much," he admitted with a yawn, "but I'd better let Joel take a squint at them before we throw them away."

7

Joel, Tony soon learned, was not available for consultation. He had gone to Paris with his father and wasn't expected back for several days.

In the meantime, the mayor came to call. Having been introduced to this dignitary by Sister Agatha, all the Nelsons knew him by sight. He arrived at ten o'clock in the morning, watching each step as he walked cautiously along the rough path. Jan saw him coming from the kitchen window. She was helping her mother pack a picnic lunch to take on their first real excursion. Now there was bound to be a delay.

Rapping on the front door, which was open, the

mayor arranged his plump face in a benign smile. *"Bonjour, madame, m'sieur,"* he said, when the Nelsons greeted him. *"Et les petites."*

Jan resented being called a little one. She drew herself up to her full height, held out her hand, and said, *"Je suis* Mademoiselle Janice," proud of her few words of French.

This effort triggered an explosion of language from the mayor, who rattled along in French for a couple of minutes before he saw the blank looks on the Americans' faces. Even Mr. Nelson was baffled by the local accent. At the first opportunity he said, "Won't you sit down?"

The mayor heaved himself into a chair while Jan held her breath, hoping it wouldn't collapse under his substantial weight. *"Excusez-moi,"* he said, smiling at everyone as he shifted to careful *lycée* English.

"We welcome you," he said, and nodded happily, pleased by this good beginning. "You plan to—reside—here?"

"Pour l'été seulement, Monsieur le Maire," Mr. Nelson replied.

Jan flinched. Her father had made a mistake, because the words provoked another burst of French, as incomprehensible as the previous monologue. She was relieved when her father held up his hand. "Please, could you speak English?" he begged.

The mayor sighed heavily, but he was game. "We welcome you," he said again. "The people of Vezelay are fearsome . . ." he began, then hesitated, looking anguished. ". . . are fearsome of another—er, incident."

Jan could tell that *incident* was a word of which he was proud. She suspected he had picked it up on television.

"The house," he continued, "is—how you say?—*insalubre?*"

"Not unhealthy, surely," said Mr. Nelson. "Unlucky, you mean?"

"Oui, oui," replied the mayor. *"L'assassin—"* He gulped twice, seeming too overcome to continue.

"We know about the murder of my uncle," said Mrs. Nelson, speaking slowly and distinctly in a no-nonsense tone of voice. "It is very sad, but—"

"Ah, oui, c'est bien triste!"

"But it all happened so many years ago."

"I knew Jacques Frechette well," the mayor informed her. "We grew up together." Choosing each word carefully, he added, "We were good friends, before the war."

"And then he was wounded," Mrs. Nelson said, trying to help him out.

The mayor nodded and tapped his forehead. "Here. It was a—a tragedy." He beamed suddenly, delighted to have found the word he was looking for.

Mr. Nelson looked the mayor in the eye. "Why do *you* think Jacques Frechette was murdered?" he asked unexpectedly.

"I do not think. No more."

"The police were certain it was not an accident?"

"An accident? *Impossible!* It was a very ugly crime, with a blunt weapon." Again the mayor seemed pleased with his choice of words, and again Jan thought: T.V. language.

Tony was listening with rapt attention, apparently hoping for an account of the killing. Instead, Mr. Nelson stood up. "It has been good to talk with you," he said to the mayor, "but I hope you will excuse us. We were just about to start off on an excursion."

"Ah, *une excursion*!" The mayor spoke approvingly. "*Avec le pique-nique.*" He rose from the chair ponderously and said his good-byes with careful courtesy.

"Do come again," said Mrs. Nelson, smiling politely, but she winked at Jan when they went back to the kitchen to finish their picnic preparations.

"You made him stop right at the good part!" Tony was complaining to his father in the next room.

"Could we, as a special favor, stop thinking about or talking about the murder for the next couple of hours?" Mr. Nelson's manner was firm, and Tony knew when to shut up.

Fifteen minutes later the Nelsons were on the road to St. Père. In the back of the Fiat were four towels, a cake of soap, and a cardboard carton of food. Mrs. Nelson carried Michelin's guide to Burgundy on her lap.

Under her shirt and shorts Jan had put on a bikini, Tony was wearing swimming trunks, and their parents wore bathing suits also. The plan was to stop first at the church in St. Père, which especially interested Mr. Nelson, because it was very early Gothic. Next they would visit the Roman ruins a few miles from town, and eventually they would swim and then picnic near the river. To Jan it sounded like a lovely day.

The church, however, failed to hold her attention for more than a short time. Compared to the basilica, it was small, and the damage to the stonework was extensive. While her mother and father admired the buttressing and discussed transitional architecture, she followed Tony across the road to a leather shop, then wandered off alone to see what else the village had to offer.

Looking in at an open door, Jan stood transfixed. The interior of a big workroom looked like a scene from a Dutch painting. At a long bench in the center of a sawdust-covered floor a man was busily fashioning wooden shoes.

Glancing up, he nodded and smiled. "*Entrez, mademoiselle.*"

Not in the least put off by the fellow's snaggle-toothed grin, or by the sawdust clinging to his eyebrows and hair that made him look like a disreputable Santa Claus, Jan walked in. One wall was lined with shelves, on which dozens of pairs of wooden shoes were ranged, large and small, wide and narrow, according to their sizes.

"*Les sabots,*" said the shoemaker proudly.

"*Sabots.*" Jan repeated the word, trying to fix it in her mind.

"*Pour vous?*" The man swung around to select a pair, but Jan backed off and shook her head.

"No, No, thank you. I'm just looking." The remark, so very American, popped out before she could help it.

"*Non?*" Quite undismayed, the shoemaker reached for the biggest pair of *sabots* on the shelves. "*Pour votre fiancé!*"

Jan began to laugh. "No *fiancé,*" she told him. With hands held more than a foot apart, she pretended to measure the shoes. "Very big."

"*Très grands,*" was the way the shoemaker expressed it. "*Pour un grand homme.*" He put the *sabots* back on the shelf and seemed sorry to see Jan leave.

When she reached the church, the rest of the family were getting into the car. "Now the ruins!" Tony exclaimed. Jan didn't know what he expected, but she could tell he was terribly disappointed when they arrived at an open field laid out in a pattern of low stone walls connected in some ancient sequence.

No building remained standing. Not even a pillar marked the place where Romans in togas or battle dress had walked and talked and bathed. One of the few recognizable relics was a sunken bath.

"What's to see here?" asked Tony grumpily. "A couple of wells, some dumb stones, and that old tub."

"I'd like to have the tub back at the cottage," said his mother.

"It would fill the whole kitchen," Jan said.

The conversation about bathing reminded her father the time had come to head for the river. He had marked a place on the map where two bridges were crisscrossed over the Cure. Parking the car near the lower bridge, he led the way along a shady footpath that bordered the broad, shallow stream. Several groups of picnickers had already staked out claims, setting up portable tables and chairs in French fashion, then settling down to an elaborate noon repast.

"They've never heard of brown bagging," Jan remarked, as the footpath disappeared, and with it the woodland. At a bend in the river there was an open field on the opposite bank.

"Let's try wading across," Mr. Nelson proposed. Pulling off his sneakers, he again led the way. Tony leaped from rock to slippery rock like a mountain goat, but Jan and her mother, carrying bags of food, were more cautious. Nobody would enjoy wet French bread.

On the grassy verge of the field, Tony and his father dumped the towels, then waded upstream to look for a pool deep enough to swim in. The water was icy, and Jan shivered at the thought of getting wet all over, but her mother was braver. As a child she had spent summers on the Maine coast.

Indeed, once the first shock was over, bathing in the river turned out to be a lark. Tossing soap from hand to hand, the Nelsons joked and teased one another, each claiming to be the cleanest. "Tony loses hands down," Mrs. Nelson said. "Look at his fingernails."

Tony reached down for a handful of sand and started to scrub the tips of his fingers just as his father stepped off a ledge into the pool they had all been hoping for. Cleanliness was immediately abandoned. Everyone went for a swim.

Drying out later on the sunny bank, Jan marveled at the fun they were having together. This summer, of course, was a very special time. There were no lessons, no dental appointments, no tennis matches or social engagements to scatter them all over Moorestown. Actually, Moorestown seemed as far away as the moon.

The house in the cherry orchard held them closely together. Even the murder of Jacques Frechette seemed to be peculiarly theirs. Jan's thoughts returned to the mayor's warning. "Is there such a thing as an unlucky house?" she wondered aloud, as she unwrapped a deviled egg.

"Not in my book," replied her father unhesitatingly. "I'm afraid the mayor is as superstitious as the rest of the villagers."

"He was trying to be kind, I think, warning us off," put in Jan's mother.

"Margot! You're not taking him seriously."

"Of course not. I suppose he's had an overdose of television."

Jan smiled. "I kept waiting for the next commercial."

"Elderly people tend to live in the past," her father remarked. "In Vezelay they can't forget this murder."

"Especially not now, when along come these crazy Americans," said Jan.

"Let's us crazy Americans exorcise the past!" Tony cried cheerfully.

"T.V. again," said Jan.

"Or horror movies," groaned her mother.

"Well, anyway," said Mr. Nelson, "we don't have to worry. You live in the future, Jan. Tony lives in the present. And your mother and I have staked out a pleasant middle-age limbo. Let's pack up and take to the road."

On the way home, by a route noted as picturesque on the map, Mr. Nelson came to a crossroad where a store advertised its wares on a brightly colored sign. Translating, he read the legend aloud. "Minerals, Honey, Candy, Jewelry, Fossils."

"Let's go see the fossils, Dad!" Tony bounced up and down. "Maybe I could sell some of the ones in the attic, if Joel thinks they're any good."

"The born opportunist," Mr. Nelson murmured, but he pulled up in front of the store.

Tony jumped out of the car and went up the short walk at a run, Jan following more sedately with her parents.

Inside the big front room of a converted dwelling were row upon row of glass cabinets, housing a heterogeneous collection of minerals and fossils, some from the local countryside, others from various parts of the world. There were chunks of amethyst from Morocco, green malachite from the Congo, hemimorphite crystals from Mexico that looked like iridescent flowers, even a combination of three minerals found at a zinc mine in Franklin, New Jersey, U.S.A.

Although Jan found the colorful minerals interesting and beautiful, Tony hurried past them to a case of fossils, pouring over those tagged as having been found nearby. Some fragments sold for a few francs, but good specimens of intact seashells or fish skeletons ran as high as a hundred francs or more, and there was a very special sea urchin that was priced at 500 francs, the equivalent of $125.

Tony's eyes grew round and covetous. "Gee, wouldn't it be neat if I could turn up something like that!" he said to Jan, running his fingers over his palm as if he were counting money.

"You're impossible," Jan told him.

"Don't you want to get rich? I do." Tony went on dreaming.

In an adjacent room, cans of honey were arranged on shelves, and a young man in a white apron was operating a modern taffy-making machine. Jan nibbled a sample piece but found the honey flavor cloying. "Too sweet," Tony agreed, and spit his into the road as the car rolled away from the shop.

For the rest of the way home, he talked about nothing but fossils. "As soon as Joel gets back from Paris, I'll have him over. He knows a lot about fossils."

The minute the Nelsons reached the cottage, Tony made for the attic, scampering up the ladder as fast as a chipmunk. Jan could hear the door scrape back with a creaking noise. Then, above her head, sounded Tony's prancing footsteps.

There was a second's silence, followed by an angry bellow. "Mom! Dad!" he yelled at the top of his lungs. "Somebody's been up here! My fossils are scattered all over the floor!"

8

Tony blamed not only himself but the entire family.

"You promised to get a proper door lock, Mom!"

"Why didn't you pull the ladder around to the cellar, Dad?"

"Jan, who did you talk to about my fossils?"

"Nobody," Jan retorted. "And they aren't *your* fossils, Tony. They're *ours*!"

"What there is left of them."

Since the box of fossils had never been looked through carefully, they couldn't tell whether anything had been taken, but Tony was convinced that he had missed the opportunity of a lifetime. To emphasize his frustration, he kicked a heavy rock and stubbed his toe. "A thief got the one piece worth selling. I just know it!"

His fury turned to disappointment, which lasted overnight. At breakfast, he looked so unhappy that his mood infected the rest of the family.

Saying, "Twice is just once too often," Mr. Nelson made a decision. "I'm going to report the incidents to the police," he said. "This harassment has got to stop."

Alone, he went to the *gendarmerie*, answering Tony's "Can't I come along?" with a definite negative.

Jan watched her father leave the house contemplatively. She felt that he would be wasting his breath, since there had been no provable robbery. If the thief had found what he was looking for, the visits would stop. But if he hadn't?

For the first time, a definite ripple of fear crept along her spine. The mayor might have been wise in warning them off. Maybe he recognized, from his long experience in the village, that they were in real danger.

The depression that seeped through the family even dampened Mrs. Nelson's usual good spirits. Helping Jan rig a clothesline between two cherry trees, she said, "Ah, for a washer dryer!"

Hanging clothes on a line for the first time in her life, Jan agreed thoroughly. After the rain, the soil was spongy and her sneakers were soon soaked. She told her mother about the *sabot* maker and said, "Wooden shoes make sense, you know. I'm going to ask how much they cost the next time we're in St. Père."

Her father arrived home about eleven o'clock, and hard on his heels came a priest, pink-cheeked and well fed, who introduced himself as Père Edmond. He had small, squinty eyes and a darting glance, which seemed to accent an unfortunate nervous tic.

Apparently, Père Edmond made a habit of calling on all new residents, but he lingered even after he had ascertained that the Nelsons were not of his faith. On and on he stayed, practicing his limited English while Mr. Nelson labored with occasional replies in French.

Père Edmond, who sat facing the kitchen door, sniffed eagerly at the fragrance of simmering soup. "Ah, *herbes de* Provence!" he said. "Madame is a gourmet cook, *n'est-ce pas*?" and would accept no negative answer. Again and again his eyes went to the kitchen door, and when Jan got up to turn down the gas flame under the pot, he licked his lips.

The clock had chimed twelve before he finally went off, in considerable disappointment. "I know he wanted to be asked for lunch," Jan whispered to her mother. "He looked positively greedy."

As Eric had warned, the news of the break-ins at the cherry orchard house spread quickly from the *gendarmerie* and raced through the village like a brush fire out of control. In the early afternoon, people began walking past the gate in twos and threes. They treated themselves to a peep show if they felt they were undetected. Even *attempted* robberies were of immediate interest to the inhabitants of Vezelay.

Undoubtedly, speculation abounded. Was the thief in their midst? If so, who was he? And where might he be expected to strike next? The mayor and the priest were popular sources of information, because they had actually paid a visit to the Americans. The Stocktons, who were known to have entertained the Nelsons, also came under considerable scrutiny.

Sister Agatha, drawn by the invisible strings of rumor, walked over from the Centre about three o'clock. Too polite to pry, she commiserated with Jan's parents. "So unfortunate. *C'est bien triste.* But if nothing of importance was taken—"

"Of that we cannot be sure," Mrs. Nelson told her. She didn't elaborate. "I'm learning," she told Jan, when the Sister had left, "to use a good deal of self-control."

Much later in the afternoon, having finished his stint at Alexandra's house, Eric stopped by. Ostensibly, he came to bring Tony what he called "a rather decent fossil" he had found when digging a new rose bed. Actually, he wanted to tell Mr. Nelson that his parents had a gun he could borrow if he felt threatened.

Because Tony was off on one of his frequent village safaris, Eric left the fossil on a windowsill and received a half-amused refusal concerning the gun. "I'd rather handle a burglar," Jan's father confessed.

Spread out on a table in the front room were all the Frechette memorabilia Jan had locked away in the trunk. Her mother was turning over old photographs, hoping she might find pictures of her uncles among them. When she came across a likeness of a man in the uniform of a French infantryman, she gave a little cry. "This could be Uncle Jacques."

Eric came to look over her shoulder, and Jan leaned closer. The soldier was slight and thin, neither handsome nor brave-looking. He was staring at the camera intently, with a see-the-birdie expression, and seemed uncomfortable.

"He would have been a very little man to murder," Jan's mother said.

"You can't be sure it's Uncle Jacques," Mr. Nelson reminded her. "See if there's any writing on the back."

There was no name, but there was a capital letter that looked like a *J* or a curlicued *S*, followed by two dates, 1910–1948.

"The dates are right, said Mrs. Nelson at once. There being no other picture of a man in uniform, she put the photograph on the mantel. Uncle Jacques he became.

She started to sort through the rest of the pile,

handling cardboard so brittle it often broke in her hands. Interested, Eric sat down beside her, and a search for Uncle Armand began.

It didn't take long. Armand had signed his name with a considerable flourish across two cabinet photographs. He was more personable than his older brother, sleek and successful-looking as he sat in a Paris photographer's armchair. The watch chain strung across his striped vest was stretched to the limit, but it was doubtless gold. He looked, as he should, like a prosperous businessman.

His handwriting intrigued Jan. The script was slanting, with curlicues on the ends of capital letters. It was the same handwriting she had admired in the copybooks, elegant and studied. Apparently, he had kept his precision from childhood until middle age.

Tony bounced into the room and immediately spotted the photograph on the mantel. He said "Hi" to Eric, then went over and examined it more closely. "Who's he?"

"We're pretty sure it's my Uncle Jacques," said his mother. She was gathering up the discarded photographs, along with a packet of letters.

"Tony, I have something for you." Eric handed him the "rather decent fossil," but the gift didn't raise his spirits much. All day he had been disconsolate, out of sorts with the world as well as with himself. "I've sort of lost interest in fossils," he admitted grumpily.

"Anyway," said Jan in an attempt to be cheerful, "the burglar didn't find any of this stuff. I locked it up in a trunk and took the key downstairs."

"I wish we'd locked up the fossils," Tony complained. "Who wants a bunch of old pictures and letters?"

"The letters might be interesting," Eric suggested. "They might even contain a clue to the cause of the murder."

Aroused, Tony said, "That's a thought. The trouble is, they're all written in French."

"I can read French," said Eric. He glanced at Mr. and Mrs. Nelson. "If you like, I'll take them home and look them over."

"That would be lovely," said Mrs. Nelson apathetically, appearing tired and distraught.

As Eric picked up the packet of letters, Tony pranced over to the mantel once more to look at the photograph closely. "Old Uncle Uglug," he said, considering. "It wouldn't have taken a very large blunt instrument."

Although he was merely expressing his mother's earlier thought in different terms, her eyes unexpectedly filled with tears. She dashed them away with the back of her hand, but not before Eric noticed.

"Excuse me," she said. "I'm a little tired." She tried to laugh. "I'm not used to doing laundry in a dishpan."

"Why don't you go lie down, Margot?" Mr. Nelson proposed, but Eric had a better idea. "Come take a walk with me. You need to get out of here. Anyway, I want to show you Alexandra's garden."

Mrs. Nelson returned home an hour later, restored and smiling. "The garden is beautiful," she said, "and Alexandra is simply marvelous. We took an instant liking to one another."

"Did she ask you in for a glass of tea?"

Jan's mother nodded, and her glance embraced the entire family. "She told the most marvelous story about Père Edmond. Obviously, he likes to eat well."

Tony patted his stomach, pretending it was a paunch, and made a face.

"Well," continued Mrs. Nelson, "it seems he assiduously visits his parishioners around the time of the first frost, when each farmer kills the pig he has raised over the summer. Apparently, he hopes to be given a choice morsel to take home for his larder." She smiled in recollection.

"Alexandra says he arrived at one farmer's house at just the right moment, rubbing his hands and saying, 'I see you've just killed the pig.' The farmer couldn't deny it, but he asked the priest a strange question. '*Mon père,* what's the difference between Jesus Christ and my pig?' While the priest pondered the farmer said, 'I'll tell you. Jesus Christ died for all mankind, but this pig—why, he died only for me.' So the priest left empty-handed."

"Just as he left here without lunch, poor fellow."

Jan's father chuckled as he spoke. "He must have many disappointments."

"Poor fellow my eye," muttered Tony. "He's just plain greedy."

By unspoken agreement, none of the Nelsons discussed either the break-in or the murder again that evening. Tony, instead of racing off as soon as he finished his dinner, helped Jan with the dishes, and Mrs. Nelson sat in the lumpy easy chair ("uneasy chair," Mr. Nelson called it) and mended a hole in her one and only cashmere sweater.

When she went to bed, Jan leafed once again through the old copybooks she had brought down from the trunk. They were interleaved with occasional snapshots–two boys fishing, a girl with long curls posing in a swing, an elderly woman wearing a bonnet that had gone out of style at the turn of the century, and a group of schoolchildren surrounding a dragonlike teacher who, although female, seemed to have a small moustache.

Jan yawned. There was nothing here of interest. A collection of trivia, her father would have described it.

Then, pasted to the inside back cover of the book she was about to toss aside, Jan found a Manila envelope stuffed with postcards. Scenic or city views in foreign countries, they were all addressed to Armand Frechette, and, from what she could make out of the postmarks, they had been sent during a fairly short period of time, no more than a year or so. They came from Brazil, Singapore, Turkey, French Guinea, East Africa, Egypt, Mauritius, Australia. Somebody had traveled fast and far.

Unfortunately, the handwriting was a lazy scrawl, almost undecipherable. Even in English the messages would have been hard to read.

Maybe Eric can make something of them, Jan thought, and saved the cards just in case. She turned out the light and settled down in bed with the faint hope that between the letters and the postcards some clue to the reason for Jacques Frechette's strange death might be found.

9

Late the next afternoon Jan decided to do some sketching. Carrying crayons, a pad of paper, and the packet of foreign postcards, she timed her departure with Eric's usual appearance on the road to Alexandra's house.

"Hi," she said cheerfully.

"Hi, there."

"Working at the Jourdans'?"

"Yeah."

Jan walked along beside him until they reached the garden door. "Have you had a chance to look over those letters?" she asked.

"Not yet."

Eric was in one of his taciturn moods, perhaps wary because they were alone. Determined to conceal her annoyance, Jan said, "I'm going around to the ramparts. When you're finished, can you spend a few minutes with me? I've got something else I'd like you to see."

Eric hesitated, apparently searching for some way out of a situation he viewed as a trap.

"Oh, forget it!" Jan said, at the end of her patience. "What's the matter with you, anyway? I won't bite." Turning on her heel, she stalked off.

With her head held high, her eyes blazing, she walked past the narthex of the basilica. I won't beg for his attention, she thought. If he finds me too young, or too tiresome, or too anything, he could at least be civil.

Taking the footpath that led around the great church to the park where the ancient chateau of the abbots had once stood, she passed a girl and a boy strolling slowly, arms around each other's waist. Her pace increased, along with her angry sense of rejection. A young man with a backpack went by, heading toward the village. He turned to look back at Jan admiringly, but she didn't notice, nor did she pay any attention to an elderly man who shuffled along near the low stone wall, spearing candy wrappers and abandoned cigarette packs—always empty—with a pointed stick.

There was a place on the wall where the view was

framed by a leafy tree limb. Jan sat down and swung around so that her back faced the park and her legs hung over the rocky slope to the valley. She turned back the cover of her sketch pad to the first blank page and slashed away with a purple crayon, outlining the jagged pattern of the fields. Her mood was purple this afternoon. Purple and red and burnt orange. The dusty yellows and greens of the ripening grain seemed too bland to reproduce.

As Jan became caught up in the process of capturing her personal view on paper, the old man with the pointed stick came by again, pausing for a moment to look over her shoulder, but she didn't notice. Even Eric's infuriating behavior had retreated to the recesses of her mind. Tourists paid no heed to the girl sketching. They came to the wall to admire the fields and hills, then turned away.

The old man came by a third time, and finally Jan saw him, deciding he must be the caretaker the Stocktons had talked about. Like the mayor and some of the other elderly residents, he had known Jacques Frechette. Sitting astride the wall now, Jan smiled and nodded, wishing she could speak French so that she could talk to him.

"*Bonjour,*" the man muttered, and regarded her appraisingly.

Does he know who I am? Jan wondered. He must. Everyone in Vezelay should be able to recognize all four of us by now.

La mademoiselle Américaine?" The elderly voice was hoarse.

"*Oui,*" Jan said.

"*Aha!*"

Was she imagining it, or was the man regarding her craftily?

Glancing around the shady park, Jan saw that they were not alone and felt more secure. Then, to her surprise, she noticed Eric on one of the diagonal gravel paths, coming toward them.

Apparently, her outburst had not put him off as thoroughly as she had expected. He said, "Hi, Jan," in a normal tone of voice, then stopped to talk to the old man in French, while Jan stuffed her grease crayons into their box and slid down from the wall, ready to start home.

"I didn't think you'd show up," said Jan, as Eric fell into step beside her.

"You said you had something to show me?"

Jan felt for the pack of postcards stuffed into the pocket of her jeans, but instead of answering she asked, "Was that the caretaker?"

Eric nodded. "His name is Dubois." He spelled it for her.

"Not a very attractive character."

"He drinks too much *vin rouge,* but he's really quite pitiful. His wife has been sick for years. The nuns take care of her as best they can, but her medicines cost a heck of a lot. He always needs money."

Eric seemed to have decided to ignore Jan's earlier irritation, and certainly she felt no need to apologize. Things said could not be unsaid, anyway. She walked along at a steady pace and in her own good time held out the postcards. "Another attic find," she said. Feeling unfriendly, she sounded so. "The handwriting is almost illegible, perhaps not worth trying to decipher."

Eric glanced at the top three or four cards. "You never can tell. Want me to go over them along with the letters?"

"If it's not too much trouble," said Jan, increasing her pace slightly.

"No trouble at all." Eric matched his stride to her quicker steps. "By the way, your mother and Alexandra have gone for a walk. I was supposed to tell you."

"They like one another," said Jan.

"Yes," agreed Eric. "I have some other news, too. The Jourdans are planning a party for the balloonists. We're all to be invited."

"You mean your family and mine?"

"Yep. Isn't that great?"

"Sounds like fun," said Jan, becoming aware of the reason for Eric's sudden shift of mood. He would have a chance to meet the balloonists.

"One of the new lot that's due next week is an old friend of Monsieur Jourdan," Eric explained. "She's an Englishwoman named Mrs. Trench, according to Alexandra."

"Has Mr. Jourdan came back from Paris?" Jan asked.

Eric nodded. "He's been back for a couple of days, but he's been working."

"Working? What does he do?"

"He writes," said Eric.

"Novels?"

"No. Newspaper and magazine pieces about antiques and collectibles. He's considered an authority on all kinds of things—Renaissance clocks, Louis Quinze furniture, coins, stamps, Chinese porcelains."

"He sounds terrifying!"

"He is, in a way," Eric replied thoughtfully. "He's so very certain of his accomplishments. Besides, he's very impressive-looking. A big man, six feet two or three, with a Vandyke beard. You'll see him around. He takes long walks, sometimes as far as Asquins and back."

"Asquins? That's the one we call the invisible village. It's in the hills, just out of sight from the cottage."

"Right. I've been meaning to tell Margot about the baker there. He's famous for his big round loaves of country bread. It makes great toast, even when it's stale."

"We'll have to try it," Jan murmured, as they approached the place where their paths divided. Eric's house lay straight downhill, while she had to cut across the square.

He could have taken the roundabout course, but instead he scarcely broke his stride when they reached the rue St. Étienne. "Bye," he said abruptly, as if his good mood had suddenly spent itself. Without even a wave of his hand, he hurried off.

Although she was growing accustomed to these sudden shifts of humor, Jan continued to resent Eric's attitude. He reared back like a frightened horse from the prospect of any prolonged conversation, no matter how impersonal.

Dawdling in the square, Jan glanced into gift-shop windows. There were replicas of pediments from the basilica, copper pots, local pottery, baskets by the score. Although she had been in Vezelay for less than a fortnight, Jan already found them without meaning. Objects to attract tourists, they had nothing to do either with village life or her own.

By the time she reached the cottage, she knew that her mother was ahead of her. From the kitchen came a rich odor of cooking, which drifted through the open window. "I never thought I'd be cooking beef Burgundy *in* Burgundy," Mrs. Nelson called, as Jan crossed the doorstep. "Well, darling, did you have a good afternoon?"

"Good enough."

"You sound disgruntled. Anything wrong?"

Since they were alone, Jan decided to be honest. "I don't understand Eric."

"What don't you understand about him?"

"He treats you and Alexandra like real people, even calls you by your first names. I've tried hard to be friendly but he shies away as if I were poison."

Mrs. Nelson turned from stirring the stew and spoke quietly. "I wouldn't stop trying if I were you."

"You would if you knew how he acts! What's wrong with me?"

"Darling, you're a girl."

"Has he got a thing about girls then? You and Alexandra were girls too."

"Were." Jan's mother laughed. "But not now. Eric feels safe with us because we're harmless."

"I'm pretty harmless myself."

"Not to Eric, at this particular time. I think he considers you a threat."

Jan tossed her sketch pad on the table and sank down, cross-legged, on the red-tiled floor. "A threat? Mother, come off it!"

"I'm serious, Jan. Somehow or other, I believe he has been hurt."

"You mean, ditched by a girl?"

"I'm only guessing," her mother replied quickly. "Eric hasn't confided in me, but there's a look in his eyes sometimes, a certain distress, even bitterness. You must have noticed it."

Jan didn't answer. She had been so self-absorbed that she hadn't thought much about Eric's feelings.

"Just try to be kind, dear. And I'll tell you one thing. If he talks to anyone about his problems, it may very well be you."

Jan was thinking about this conversation the next afternoon as she walked back to the ramparts in the basilica park. She wanted to sketch the same scene again, but in less flamboyant colors. Her mother's advice had been sobering. Today she would work with yellows and browns and greens.

As she turned out of the orchard gate a man came striding down the hill, and Jan knew at once that he could be nobody but Monsieur Jourdan. Eric's description had been apt. He was big and impressive, with a gait that belied his age and a cane used more as an ornament than a crutch. His head was large and so were his hands, but they were in proportion to his unusual height. When he passed Jan, he gave her a quick glance and smiled slightly, but he didn't speak.

Trudging uphill, Jan happened to glance down at the road, and there, just visible in the loose gravel, was the imprint of Monsieur Jourdan's shoe. A huge shoe!

Glancing behind her to be sure she was unobserved, Jan impulsively knelt and measured the imprint with her sketch pad, marking the length and width with a crayon hastily pulled out of the box. She was back on her feet in a few seconds, and by the time she turned into the churchyard she began to feel foolish. What had possessed her? There was no possible reason to suspect Alexandra's rich and famous husband of buying a ladder and carting it down through the tangled cherry orchard in order to enter the cottage attic by stealth.

Still, the man who had done so had big feet, perhaps as big or bigger than Monsieur Jourdan's. She had acted childishly, but so what? Equally childishly, she intended to check her measurement with the outline in the attic. Then she could forget the whole thing.

Passing the apse of the basilica, with its sturdy buttresses, Jan cut across the grass to the place on the wall where she had been working the day before. The light was different, because cumulus clouds laid shifting shadows on the fields, and Jan's interest quickened. Although the view was the same, the whole atmosphere had changed.

As before, she swung her legs over the wall so that she could face her subject directly. Thoughts of Eric and Monsieur Jourdan dropped from her mind. Sketching always absorbed her, shutting out the world for long stretches of time.

Yet she was aware peripherally of the trash collector coming by to empty the park's refuse cans, and when she turned her head to follow the flight of a bird she noticed the mayor strolling by, arm in arm with Père Edmond. The tourists who came and went were all strangers. They didn't count. And today Eric didn't appear, but that didn't matter. The sketch began to please Jan as it developed under her fingers. The loopy shadows softened the sharp edges of the fields, and the blue-and-white sky gave all the color interest she need for contrast.

From the bell tower five musical notes reached her ears. Behind her a child scampered along the path, calling to his companion. The park was emptying, the tourists heading back to their cars and buses, but Jan was insensible to their retreat.

Holding the sketch pad at arm's length with her left hand, she examined her drawing, then looked out over the panorama before her. Not bad, she thought, and her pulse quickened. Would she dare to show this sketch to Mrs. Stockton and ask for her criticism?

This was the last thing Jan remembered clearly. A heavy thud on her back knocked the sketch pad from her hand. At the same instant, she flew from the parapet as though shot from a catapult. Then she was falling, falling, down through the scrub growth that clung to the hillside until she crashed agonizingly against a precipitous, rocky slope.

Jan tried to scream, but her voice betrayed her.

Blood from a cut on her forehead drenched her eyes. Hot stabs of pain attacked her like biting wolves. She blanked out, mercifully unconscious as she tumbled over and over, like a doll flung into a ravine. A scree of stones followed in her wake.

10

The X-ray table was cold and hard. Jan, still in shock, lay rigid under the hood of the instrument that was photographing her spine. The technician briskly turned her to her right side and moved her left hip, placing her thigh at a right angle to her body.

"*Correctement.*"

Jan was dimly aware of a young face, straight hair pulled back and caught in a barette, a white jacket. The girl went out of the room and called something in French. Jan supposed she was meant to lie still. As the machine whirred briefly, she tried not to breathe.

"*Fini,*" said the technician, coming back for the

last of the X-ray plates. She smiled, nodded, and disappeared.

Alone, Jan tried to organize the scattered thoughts that pulsed in her brain.

What had happened? Why had she fallen? Could her back be broken? The final question terrified her. She lay and fretted.

Suppose the summer was ruined, and it was all her fault?

What had become of her mother and father? Why weren't they with her? She remembered vaguely the trip to the hospital. They had been with her then.

Jan also was aware that the hospital was in Avallon. It lay behind grilled iron gates off the market square, a great old building that looked like a huge private house. Inside, however, it was as modern and antiseptic as a hospital in the United States.

After a long time, the technician returned with a doctor, who examined the X-ray pictures against a strong light. He patted Jan's arm and went into an adjoining room, treading silently on rubber soles. At last she could hear her parents' voices! Some of the tension drained away, but there was a catch in her breath as she sighed.

A man in a blue-cotton hospital coat came in. "*Bon soir,*" he said pleasantly, and helped the technician transfer Jan from the X-ray table to a rolling stretcher, which terrified her. Were they going to operate?

That fear was quickly dispelled, because he wheeled her down a hall and through the door into a small room furnished with a high hospital bed. Every now and then he spoke encouragingly, bobbing his head, across which a few strands of gray hair were carefully combed. Then, to Jan's embarrassment, the man undressed her, pulling her blood-caked shirt gently over her head and talking in a steady stream of French as he removed one article of clothing after another and helped her put on a wrinkled white cotton garment that tied in the back.

To move her from the stretcher to the bed, he called in another nurse. Jan gritted her teeth in an effort not to groan. She felt bruised and beaten. Her bandaged forehead throbbed, her back ached, and her assaulted dignity added to her wretchedness.

As soon as the stretcher was wheeled away, Jan's parents came into the room. "Darling, you're going to be all right," her mother said at once, looking more relieved than stricken. "The X-rays showed clearly that there's no fracture. You're a lucky girl."

"I don't feel lucky," said Jan, as her father came over and took her hand. "I hurt."

"Of course, you do," her father said. "You had a terrible fall." He looked pale and drawn, as if he had been through a very bad time himself.

Jan turned her head slowly toward her mother. "What kind of hospital is this? That man who just left *undressed* me!"

"He's a male nurse, dear. At home, female nurses undress men. Nobody thinks anything of it."

"He's called an *infermier,*" said her father.

Neither of her parents troubled Jan with questions. They simply told her that the doctor in charge had decided she needed a couple of days of bed rest while the healing process began.

"You mean I've got to stay here all alone?"

"We'll come to see you every day and bring Tony," her father promised.

"He's staying with the Stocktons until we get back," her mother told her.

Jan was too concerned with her own predicament to pay much attention. How did they dare abandon her in a strange hospital in a foreign country? "I can't understand a word they say," she muttered unhappily.

"But you'll be much more comfortable here," her father said.

"What time is it?" Jan asked. For the first time she realized that the window in the room was a dark rectangle.

"After nine o'clock."

"They'll give you a pill to ease the pain and put you to sleep." Her mother's voice was intended to be comforting.

"You're in good hands, Jan. It's a very nice little hospital."

Nice! As though any hospital could be nice. Jan looked at her father dubiously as her mother bent to kiss her.

"Good night, darling."

"Good night."

Forsaken, Jan lay flat on her back and allowed a few salt tears to well out of her eyes and dribble back to her ears, where they felt cold and tickly. Then she pulled herself together and obediently swallowed two pills a nurse brought her.

The nurse stayed long enough to explain the mechanics of the room in sign language. By pressing a button, Jan could turn out her light. By pressing another one, she could call for help. There was a radio in her bedside table and a private bathroom lined with flowered tiles, but she was not aware of these conveniences until morning. The moment she was alone she became drowsy, and in a few minutes she was fast asleep.

When it was barely light, the door to Jan's room opened and a cheerful voice said, *"Bonjour, mademoiselle."*

"Bonjour," Jan replied sleepily, and opened her eyes experimentally as she was handed a cereal bowl filled with a caramel-colored liquid. *"Café au lait,"* the uniformed kitchen helper said.

Café au lait. An elegant-sounding name for a simple and rather uninteresting drink, which was not improved by being lukewarm. With it came two pieces of dry toast, no fruit juice, no egg. Jan swallowed a little of the sweetened coffee and milk, munched on a piece of the toast, and felt sorry for herself.

After a while, a nurse came in and helped her into the bathroom. Every muscle, every joint, every tendon complained, but after she had stood under a hot shower for several minutes the discomfort lessened. Once back in a freshly made bed, she even felt refreshed. The pain, although still severe, was more bearable. Only when she tried to move did Jan wince. Lying quite still, she found she could think, and she had a lot to think about.

This morning she could recall the blow that had sent her spinning off the wall quite clearly. Whether she had been struck or pushed she didn't know, but she was sure that someone had deliberately attacked her.

When a nurse came in to take her temperature, Jan felt strong enough to indicate that she wanted pencil and paper. *Papier*, she could manage, but the word for pencil slipped her mind, so she made a writing motion in the air. The nurse nodded. "*Crayon*," she said, smiling.

When a pad of paper and a rather stubby pencil arrived, Jan thanked the nurse warmly. Then she raised herself cautiously up on the pillows and began to make a list, using headings and subheadings as though she were outlining a high-school theme.

People Who Knew Jacques Frechette:

1. The mayor.*
2. The trash collector.*
3. Junot, the farmer.
4. Dubois, the caretaker at the church.
5. Père Edmond, the greedy priest.*
6. Monsieur Jourdan?

After the names of the mayor, priest, and trash collector she put stars, because they had been in the park yesterday afternoon and could have noticed her sketching on the parapet. Jan considered for a few minutes, then added a final subheading.

7. Others?

Of the 300-odd people in the village there must have been others who were acquainted with the murdered man, but how she could seek them out Jan had no idea. After a while, she made a new heading.

Possible Treasure:

1. Coin or coins from the old mint.
2. Real money.
3. Rare fossil. (Unlikely, since if fossil was

stolen, no point in attacking me to scare us off.)

4. Letter or letters that might identify murderer or name treasure.
5. Something unknown, but valuable.

What, conceivably, could the fifth item be? Something small certainly, if it was still in the house. Otherwise, something buried in the cellar, or in the orchard, in which case the chance of its discovery was slim indeed.

Jan discarded this last idea as unreasonable. Somebody firmly believed that the treasure was still in the house and probably hidden in the attic. Otherwise, why the break-ins?

At that moment there was a knock on the door. Jan slipped the pad under the bed sheet and called, "Come in!" expecting her parents. To her utter astonishment, Eric appeared, carrying a small bunch of field poppies.

He looked at Jan anxiously. "How are you feeling?"

Instead of answering, Jan asked some questions herself. "Why aren't you working? How did you get here?"

"I hitched," replied Eric, and held out the poppies. "How are you feeling?" he asked again.

"Better, thanks." Jan took the poppies and held

them under her nose, but they had no fragrance. Not that it mattered. She was touched and pleased. Turning painfully, she reached for a glass of water on the bedside table, the only container available. "They're beautiful," she said.

"Wait a minute!" Eric took a folder of matches from his pocket. "We ought to burn the stems. Then they'll last for days."

Patiently, one by one, he seared each slender stem and put them in water. "When I found you," he said, "I thought you were dead." The relief in his voice was unmistakable.

"You found me?"

Eric nodded, glancing up briefly from the poppies. "I wanted to tell you about the letters, so I came to the place on the wall where you sat before. Your crayons were there, but you had disappeared." He frowned and added, "Then I saw your sketch pad, halfway down the hill."

Jan waited for a moment, then said, "Go on."

"You're sure you're up to this?"

"Quite sure."

"I couldn't see any sign of you at first through the scrub growth below the wall. Then I caught a glimpse of that red shirt you wear so much."

So he had noticed! Jan's heart lifted.

"I scrambled down on those thick ropes of ivy. You can bet I was plenty scared. When I reached you, I wished I'd gone for help. Honestly, Jan, I wasn't fooling when I said I thought you were dead." Eric looked at her intently, as though he couldn't quite believe even now that she was living and breathing.

"Then what?" Jan asked.

"I tried to climb back up the hill, but I kept slipping. There were a few tourists still walking in the park, so I guess I started yelling, because they came over and looked down at me as if I'd lost my mind. Finally they got the message. I sent one fellow to look for a doctor and another one to find your parents." Clearly Eric was still upset.

"After that everything happened in slow motion. While I skidded down the hill again I guess half the village was alerted, because pretty soon a station wagon pulled up on the lower road and your father got out, along with a Dr. Deluc from Avallon who just happened to be in Vezelay and a couple of carpenters who had been working at the mayor's house. They brought along a board and lifted you onto it, explaining that it wasn't as good as a stretcher, but they didn't want to wait for an ambulance to be sent from Avallon."

"Where was my mother all this time?"

"She was with the men, but your father persuaded her to stay down by the wagon. That hill is a terror! He didn't want to risk a second catastrophe."

"My back isn't broken," Jan said.

"I know. That's some cut you've got on your forehead, though."

Jan raised a hand and touched the bandage on her forehead lightly. "I wonder if it will leave a scar?"

"I doubt it. The cut's almost on a line with your eyebrow. Besides, Dr. Deluc is very skillful, and in a pinch there's always plastic surgery."

"I can't say you're much of a comfort." Jan pretended to shudder, then smiled weakly.

Suddenly contrite, Eric asked, "Am I tiring you? Should I leave?"

"No, please!" Jan tried to look more alert as a nurse came in to take her blood pressure, then stayed to have a short conversation in French with Eric.

"She says you're doing just fine," he reported, "so I'll tell you about Armand's letters. Some were from business people in Paris, but several were from Jacques, written while he was apparently traveling around the world in 1947."

"I thought he was poor!"

"So did I, but somehow he must have acquired a big sum of money. He wrote postcards from some pretty out-of-the-way places, and a rather curious letter or two."

"Curious?"

Eric nodded. "In one, postmarked from Mauritius, he said that when he got home he'd have a surprise for the old man."

"What old man?"

Eric spread his hands. "Who knows?"

"The 'old man' couldn't have been his own father?"

"That's not an expression the French use," Eric said. "There's another letter that will interest you, Jan. It seems to indicate that there really was something hidden, and that one person in Vezelay knew what but not where."

"Of course—that one person isn't named?"

Eric shook his head.

"Just our luck." Jan sighed. "Were all the postcards from Jacques?"

"Every last one. He didn't bother to sign them, probably because Armand would recognize his scrawl."

"I wish we knew more about Jacques' personality." Jan was wondering whether he was mentally unstable or merely headstrong.

"One thing's sure," said Eric. "He was positively gloating at being off on his own."

"Where are the letters and postcards now?"

"At our house."

"Keep them there," Jan said.

"By the way, my folks send their love and sympathy. They were shocked by the news of the accident."

"Accident? Eric, it was no accident."

"What are you talking about?"

"Something, or somebody, hit my back—hard."

"Are you sure?"

"Positive."

"Why, that's terrible. Attempted burglary is one thing, but an out-and-out attack—your father will pack you off fast, and I can't say I blame him."

The color drained from Jan's face. As Eric leaned toward her in concern, she put out a hand. "Dad needn't know. Please don't tell him!" she begged.

"Jan, you can't ask that of me. The risk is too great."

For more than a minute, Jan didn't speak. She enjoyed having her hand held and was comforted by Eric's solicitude. Then she said earnestly, "I want to stay until we clear up this mystery. Somebody is determined to scare us away from the cottage, somebody who's determined to find whatever is hidden there. But I don't think that person wants to hurt any of us seriously. Eric, I don't want to leave!" She squeezed his hand hard, then pulled away and settled back on the pillows.

A nurse who hadn't appeared before came to the door. She looked starched and authoritative. "*Bonjour,*" she said, and immediately asked Eric a question. He stood up at once and turned to Jan. "If I'm not a member of the family, I must come during visiting hours," he said, as the nurse left. "Not that I didn't know it," he added in a whisper.

"How will you get home?"

"I'll ramble around the market until I find a shopper from Vezelay. Easy!" He leaned down, kissed

Jan lightly on the cheek, and went away, shutting the door behind him.

Jan smiled to herself at the unexpectedness of Eric's kiss, then settled back on the pillow. Insulated from the noise of the hallway, the room was very quiet. After a while she dozed, awakening only when her family arrived an hour later.

Tony sidled into the room gingerly, several steps behind his parents, and stood against a wall. He looked less robust than usual this morning. His size seemed to wax and wane, according to the way he was feeling, confident or unequal to the situation. Wary of the hospital atmosphere and alarmed by the bandage on Jan's forehead, he lacked his customary poise. "Hi," was all he could manage to say.

Jan grinned. "What's the matter? Lost your cool?"

Then she looked at her mother and father, who were standing together on one side of the bed. She wanted to reach up and hug them, but she was still too stiff and sore.

"Better this morning, darling?"

"Much better, Mother. I even had a shower."

"Lucky you," said Tony, recovering. He went over to the window and looked out. "Hey, the market's right outside the gates. Whaddaya know!"

Jan could feel the relief her improvement gave her parents, but she didn't want to be asked questions about her fall. Fortunately, the conversation was desultory, unimportant hospital talk with everyone wanting to be cheerful and comforting.

"When do you think they'll let me go home?" she asked, when the time seemed ripe.

"That's up to Dr. Deluc," said Jan's father. "He'll be in later."

"It's not too bad here, is it?" her mother asked soothingly.

"On the contrary, it's rather fun," Jan said, "or will be, when I stop hurting."

"Where did the flowers come from?" asked Tony unexpectedly.

"Eric brought them. He stopped by a little while ago." Jan didn't pursue the subject.

Her mother had brought a toothbrush, a comb and brush, and a couple of paperbacks, which Jan accepted gratefully. When they were ready to leave, her parents kissed her good-bye but Tony hung back awkwardly. "Don't get into any more trouble," he said in parting.

No sooner had the family left than Jan's lunch tray arrived on a cart wheeled along the hall by a kitchen helper. *"Du vin?"* the woman asked routinely.

"Non, merci," Jan said. What was the word for milk? *"Du lait?"*

Success! A carton of milk arrived in due course, and Jan hungrily attacked a small bird that might have been a pigeon, served on a bed of rice. The sauce was good, the accompanying salad fresh and green. The French certainly are good cooks, she thought, even in hospitals.

Jan waited until the tray was carried away, then settled back with one of the paperbacks. She had turned only a few pages when a dark bulk appeared in the open doorway. Looking up, she encountered a totally unexpected visitor, Père Edmond!

Crossing himself as he entered the room, the priest said, "*Bonjour, mademoiselle.*"

"*Bonjour,*" Jan replied, but instinctively drew back. She didn't like this man. She didn't even trust him. Along with the mayor, he had been in the park yesterday afternoon.

What was he doing here? Visiting the sick, of course. Jan had seen the rusty black of his cassock as he entered the room across the hall, but she hadn't caught a glimpse of his crafty face.

"*Allez-vous bien?*" Père Edmond asked. The words sounded automatic. If he had looked at her closely, Jan thought, he might have recognized her, but his eyes seemed fixed on the wall behind the bed.

"*Je ne comprends pas,*" Jan replied, hoping she was getting the phrase right. She didn't lower her book and did her best to sound discouraging.

The priest blessed her and backed out, murmuring something in French that was lost in the clatter of the hallway. Jan, whose free hand had been edging toward the call button, was relieved when he disappeared. Could it have been Père Edmond who pushed me off the wall? she was wondering. Could it conceivably have been he?

11

Jan was discharged from the hospital at noon the next day, after Dr. Deluc inspected the cut on her forehead and replaced the bandage with one that looked positively dainty.

Wearing clean clothes, Jan walked carefully to the car on her father's arm. The blood-caked red shirt and white shorts were buried at the bottom of a shopping bag.

To her surprise and delight, Jan's arrival home was pleasantly festive. Alexandra came with a big bunch of roses and told Jan that she looked interestingly pale and very feminine. "You must get strong soon, though," she said. "Soon enough to come to our party for the balloonists!" Eric's mother brought an apple tart and Sister Agatha appeared with sympathy and two glasses of local grape jelly. Even the mayor stopped by to say welcome home.

Jan regarded the mayor with more than her previous interest. He looked harmless enough, but was he? She had become suspicious of everyone who had known Jacques Frechette.

The nagging question of her attack aside, Jan quickly became aware that the attitude of the villagers had changed. When she began to take short walks, people smiled and called a greeting. The storelady in the postcard shop deserted waiting tourists to pay her special attention, and the owner of the *charcuterie* treated her like an old friend.

To the rest of the Nelsons, the villagers were equally hospitable, as though Jan's misfortune had altered the temper of the town and drawn its residents together in a protective circle. They might tolerate attempted theft, might be suspicious of American intentions, but they would not willingly permit violence in their midst. That they suspected violence rather than an accidental fall Jan had not the slightest doubt.

Oddly, Jan's parents and brother apparently discounted evil intent. They assumed she had become dizzy, warned her against such precarious heights, and let it go at that. Jan wasn't forced either to evade their questions or fabricate plausible answers, which was a great relief.

Joel, who arrived back from Paris on the same day Jan was discharged from the hospital, came over to see Tony's fossils after breakfast one morning. Although still professing disinterest, Tony took him up to the attic at once, and their shrill young voices drifted down to Jan in the room below.

Unlike Tony, Joel was a systematic boy, oriented toward things rather than people. Since there was a long period of quiet, he presumably turned each rock in his hands before he put it aside. "These three are worth saving," he said finally. "You can chuck the rest."

"What could I get for the three of them, d'you think?" Jan heard Tony ask.

"Get?"

"What would they sell for?"

Joel quietly considered the question. Jan smiled to herself as the silence lengthened.

"That man who runs the fossil store, over in the valley," Tony persisted. "Do you think he'd buy them?"

"I really don't know," Joel replied. "I never thought of selling fossils. What's the matter? Don't you like them?"

Jan repeated the interchange to her mother later

in the day. "Tony's getting downright embarrassing," she said. "All he can think of is making money."

"Poor boy, he's still searching for treasure," Mrs. Nelson said. "He knows I'd love to be able to keep this place, and he dreams childish dreams of making it possible."

Privately Jan was dreaming of the same thing, but her hopes were pinned on solving the mystery. Still, her progress seemed to have come to a standstill.

That same evening, however, Eric came over to the house with the two important letters from Jacques to his brother. Her parents were going for a stroll, and Tony was out somewhere with Joel, so Jan was able to talk to him alone.

Besides the letters he had also brought her sketch pad, and she seized the opportunity to ask him to measure the footprint outlined on the attic floor against her crayon marks.

"Way off," Eric said, when he came back down the ladder. "These marks are at least three inches shorter and a couple of inches narrower." He looked at her quizzically. "Whose shoe did you measure, anyway?"

Jan wouldn't tell him. "It doesn't matter. Let's get to the letters." She moved over on the bench under the grape arbor so that he could sit down.

The letter from Mauritius offered no clue whatever to the identity of the "old man." The second one was more interesting but equally puzzling. Eric translated the difficult scrawl haltingly.

" 'Don't waste time cleaning house. You won't—find—anything of value.' " Here Eric stopped and frowned. *" 'J'*—or is it *L—seul, connaît ce que c'est.' J*, only, knows what it is. Or the letter could be *L* or even *I*."

"Let's take it inside and look at it under a good light," Jan proposed.

By studying both Mauritius letters, placed side by side, the pair made a few deductions. Since the third person singular of the verb to know was used, Jacques couldn't be referring to himself, so it was important to be fairly certain of the capital letter.

"I'm no handwriting expert," Eric said. "What's your guess, Jan?"

After studying the two sheets of paper, Jan said, "I think it's an *L*. Look at the way he shapes a *J*, here and here and here. It's quite different."

"I'll buy that. I'll also bet the *L* stands for a first name."

"Why?"

"Well, I've read a lot of letters from Jacques Frechette. Let's just say that I'm getting to know his style."

Jan leaned on an elbow. "Do you think he was crazy?"

"No, I don't. He was a cocky little fellow, though. And I'll wager he could be pretty objectionable."

Jan agreed, but at the moment she was thinking about her list of people who had known her mother's uncle. "Do you know the mayor's first name?" she asked Eric.

Hooting, he cried, "You aren't suspecting—"

"I'm not suspecting anyone. I just asked you a question."

"His name's Laurent," Eric said.

"What about the farmer, Junot?"

"Not the vaguest." Eric said. "But it would be easy enough to find out."

"And the caretaker at the basilica?" Jan continued. "The one you call Dubois."

"He has the improbable name of Lothaire."

"Another *L*? Oh, dear! Are you on first-name terms with the trash collector?"

" 'Fraid not." Eric hesitated. "Now wait! His name is Victor—Victor Bris.

"Count him out," murmured Jan. "How about Alexandra's husband?"

"Everybody knows Lionel Jourdan. Oh, no, another L! But I doubt if Jacques would have confided in him or even been acquainted with him." Eric smiled.

"Do priests have first names?" Jan wondered aloud. "I suppose they're usually Biblical."

Eric couldn't help her out on that score, and he teased her gently. "What are you going to do, make a list of all the villagers whose first names begin with *L* and invite them up to the attic for a treasure hunt?"

"It might not be such a bad idea." Jan tried to look serious. "We could give blunt instruments as favors."

"Your macabre sense of humor does not amuse me," Eric scolded. He got up to leave, tucking the two letters back in his pocket, and looked very stern.

"Sorry," said Jan. "I'll try to be more amusing at Alexandra's party. I hope it will be a lovely day."

Her hope was realized on the following Saturday when a pink sunrise spread to light a cloudless blue sky. The balloonists were scheduled to get off the ground early and land in time to arrive at the Jourdans' house for lunch. Jan put on a dress for the occasion, the first she had worn since coming to Vezelay. She felt rather proud of the way she looked. Her hair was clean and glossy, her eye make-up becoming, and her skin discreetly tanned. There was still a small bandage over her left eyebrow, but by now she considered it a battle scar and secretly even was proud of it.

For this rather special party, the Jourdans' lawn had been partially covered by a pink-and-white striped canopy, from the supports of which great bunches of toy balloons waved in the light breeze.

Folding chairs had been set up around circular tables with pink tablecloths, laid for lunch in advance. When the Nelsons arrived, waiters in white jackets were busy passing champagne.

"Wow," commented Tony, genuinely impressed.

"Sh!" said Jan.

Alexandra was wearing pink to match the decor, in fascinating contrast to her orange hair. She was receiving guests with her husband, who looked like a huge, amiable grizzly bear standing next to a toy poodle. When Jan was introduced, he took her small hand in his big one. "I am glad you have recovered from your accident."

Jan murmured a polite answer and moved on into the garden, staying close to her mother, whose easy manner made her feel at home. The guests, apart from the balloonists, were friends of the Jourdans from Vezelay and the surrounding villages, many of them Parisians who regularly summered nearby.

There were also a few people Jan recognized, a distinguished violinist who lived next to the old mint, a young couple who ran a shop selling handwoven woolens, the ubiquitous mayor, and the manager of the hotel.

The Stocktons were at the far end of the lawn, talking English to a bevy of balloonists. Attracted to their native language like steel filings to a magnet, the Nelsons walked over and were introduced.

Jan listened to the conversation, brisk, animated, and totally concerned with the beauties of Burgundy as seen from a balloon. She stood a little apart from the rest, watching Eric, who obviously was fascinated by Mrs. Trench, the guest of honor. A sturdy woman, wearing sensible shoes and a khaki skirt paired with a rather conspicuous shirt printed with bright balloons, she seemed very much in command of the situation. "This is my fourth summer of ballooning here," Jan heard her say, "but unfortunately, in other years, my friend Lionel has been out of town."

A waiter with a laden tray was approaching. Offered a glass of champagne, Jan wondered if she dared take one. Since neither of her parents were watching, she took the chance and found that the bubbly liquid tasted rather like ginger ale, but with more flavor.

Tony had sought out Joel, who was talking to another boy of about the same age. The three went off to perch high on the stone steps and look down on the throng. They seemed pleased to be present at a grown-up party, but more comfortable by themselves, and each carried a soft drink, which they sipped straight from the bottle, disdaining the skinny-stemmed glasses they had been offered.

Edging closer to Eric, but staying out of his line of vision, Jan unobtrusively listened to his conversation with Mrs. Trench. "If I hear of an opening, I'll let you know," she was saying. "Don't count on a thing, dear boy, but give me your name and telephone number, just in case."

Eric had come prepared. He took a card from his jacket pocket and handed it to her. "You're very kind."

"And now," said Mrs. Trench in her forthright manner, "I really must go find my host. We have a mutual interest in philately."

The guests began drifting toward the tent, where Alexandra had arranged place cards on the luncheon tables. Mrs. Trench was seated on the right of Monsieur Jourdan, while Alexandra claimed the distinguished violinist. The balloonists were distributed among the guests according to whether they spoke English or only French, and Jan found herself with a lively Irishman, along with Mr. and Mrs. Stockton. Eric was seated at a table some distance away.

She wouldn't have arranged things this way, but she accepted the situation with good grace. Tony and his companions, carrying heaping plates, had again staked out their territory at the top of the steps, and Eric seemed contented with his balloonist.

White wine, a Pouilly Fumé from the region, was served at lunch, and Jan was thirsty. She began to feel very happy, talking and laughing more than usual, and was unaware that when a waiter started to refill her glass Mrs. Stockton waved him off.

Dessert was a chocolate mousse, and Jan suddenly lost her appetite. "Do you think I might be excused?" she asked Mrs. Stockton, who was on her left.

"Of course, dear. Are you feeling all right?"

"Yes, thank you." Jan put down her napkin, got up, smiled brightly at everyone, and walked away, mounting the steps from the garden on the opposite side from the three boys. She was in a hurry now, but she climbed carefully, hoping to locate a bathroom without asking for help.

Cutting through the living room, the only part of the house with which she was familiar, Jan entered a long hall with doors closed, in the French fashion, on either side. Cautiously she opened one after another, coming to a paneled library and then to the equivalent of an American powder room.

She was just in time. As she locked the door behind her Jan broke out in a cold perspiration, then was immediately and violently sick at her stomach.

The champagne. The wine. Jan knew at once what was wrong, but she was heartsick at such an ending to a sophisticated party. She bathed her face with a guest towel wrung out in cold water and blessed the fact that at least she hadn't disgraced herself in public. Then she heard voices next door!

Monsieur Jourdan was talking with Mrs. Trench, whose speech was as recognizable as her manner. "My dear Lionel," she was saying, "you are a great connoisseur, but you are not a serious philatelist.

You acquire rarities, but you spread yourself too thin and become involved in too many fields. Take that German clock on the mantel. Renaissance, I suppose. One of a kind. Isn't that why you bought it?"

Jan could hear Monsieur Jourdan's throaty laugh. "You have me sized up very neatly, Pamela, but I didn't bring you here to discuss fourteenth century clocks." A drawer opened and closed. "Here's something that may interest you, since you *are* a philatelist, and a famous one."

There was a period of silence lasting perhaps half a minute, then a gasp of surprise from Mrs. Trench. "But it's unique!"

"Of course. The only one in the world."

"And it must have cost you a small fortune!"

"Enough." Monsieur Jourdan chuckled.

"Do you want to sell it?"

"Heavens, no, my dear lady. I'm a collector, not a tradesman."

"Well, if you ever do, put it up for auction at Christie's," advised Mrs. Trench, not in the least discountenanced. "Much as I'd love to own it, my means are insufficient for such a treasure as this."

Treasure. The word was spoken so softly that it barely penetrated the bathroom wall, but it rang in Jan's mind like a bell. She leaned weakly against the sink until she heard the library door close and the voices fade away.

Still nauseated, Jan had no desire to return to the

party and decided to escape through the back of the house if she could find her way. The hall outside the bathroom was empty. The library door (she tried the handle!) was locked. Sounds of kitchen activity beckoned from somewhere to the left, so she turned in that direction.

Edging past a couple of waiters carrying steaming pots of coffee, she went through a pantry to the back door, which opened on a porch almost as high as the wall. Steps led to a cobbled yard and the servants' entrance.

Head bent, Jan clung to the railing and tottered down, stopping only briefly when she saw, neatly placed beside the bottom step, an enormous pair of French *sabots*.

Monsieur Jourdan's obviously. Jan hurried through the gate and on toward home, still weak and uncertain of her footing. The cottage was empty, of course, and she collapsed on her bed, falling asleep immediately. She awakened sometime later to the sound of her name being called.

"Jan, where are you?"

"In here, Eric."

"May I come in?"

"I guess so." Jan sat up, lifted her tangled hair from the back of her neck, and slipped her feet into the sandals she had worn to the party.

"What's wrong?" asked Eric, as soon as he took a good look at her. "Aren't you feeling well?"

"Not very," Jan admitted unhappily. "I think I had too much to drink."

"Champagne?"

Jan nodded. "Only two glasses." Her voice was tremulous. "But then there was the wine at lunch, and I guess I lost count."

Eric shook his head. "Next thing you know you'll end up a wino like Dubois."

"Don't tease me, please!"

"Poor girl." Eric's amusement turned to pity. "Were you really sick?"

"You betcha!" Jan confessed.

"Well, you did the right thing, to come home. I saw you sitting beside my mother at lunch. Then suddenly you were gone."

"I think your mother knew I was feeling ill." Jan was worried.

"She's pretty sharp," said Eric with a grin, "but she's also quite understanding."

"I wish I'd been with my own folks. Dad never would have let me."

"You can't keep your father at your elbow all your life, Jan," Eric said heartlessly, although in a commiserating tone of voice.

Jan only heard the words. "I know. I know." She twisted around and buried her head in the pillow, thoroughly ashamed of herself.

"Buck up, Jan." Eric stroked her shoulder gently. "We've all been through it."

She gave a long sigh, then abruptly sat up. "Eric, what's a philatelist?"

"Don't you know?"

"If I did, I wouldn't ask. It sounds something like a philanthropist."

"You're way off. A philatelist is a stamp collector."

"A stamp collector." Jan turned to Eric in slow motion. "Did you know that Monsieur Jourdan collects rare stamps?"

Eric shrugged. "No, but I'm not surprised."

"While I was in the bathroom," Jan said, "he was in the library next door. He was showing a stamp to that English balloonist, Mrs. Trench. She called it a treasure."

12

A treasure!

Jan awakened earlier than usual the next morning and lay wondering whether she had stumbled on a clue at last. A man whose first name began with *L* knew Jacques Frechette's secret. This man must have been a friend, not simply an acquaintance. If he were still alive, might he be persuaded to talk?

Jan didn't boggle at asking Eric's help. Since his visit to the hospital, she recognized that their relationship had changed for the better. She felt no strain when they were together. Although there was no romantic involvement, they seemed to be becoming friends at last.

Since Eric spoke French, and since he didn't work on Sundays, he was quite willing to fall in with Jan's plan and try to question the men on her list who had known Jacques Frechette and whose first names began with *L*. Together they roamed the rue St. Étienne, accosting the mayor as he walked home from church.

Because the French never liked to attack a subject directly, Eric was tactful and cautious. To Jan, the conversation seemed to go on interminably, but it yielded some results.

Jacques, according to the mayor, had changed drastically after the war, becoming so secretive and withdrawn that most people considered him unbalanced. Then he had disappeared for almost a year, telling everyone in the village that he was going around the world. Jacques, who could hardly make ends meet! He still made this preposterous claim after his reappearance. A few months later the murder took place.

Eric told Jan the mayor claimed to know nothing about hidden treasure or of any interest Jacques had displayed in postage stamps. "You might talk to Lothaire Dubois, though," he had suggested to Eric. "They saw quite a lot of each other toward the end."

The caretaker always stayed close to the basilica on Sunday mornings. Jan and Eric found him sitting on a stone bench near the south wall, taking a nip from a bottle concealed in a paper bag. He regarded

Jan mistrustfully, but was unexpectedly loquacious when Eric approached him. From an occasional word caught here and there, Jan gathered that he was discussing his family troubles, but when Eric introduced the name of Jacques Frechette, he shook his head and looked glum.

Suspecting that her presence made the caretaker wary, Jan wandered back to the square and waited for Eric there. More than fifteen minutes passed before he appeared, looking puzzled and rather uneasy. "Lothaire opened up a bit after you left," he said. "Apparently, Jacques bragged that he had a valuable piece of paper stashed away in the cottage, something the richest man in Vezelay would pay good money for, but he'd never say where it was actually hidden. Not to Lothaire, anyway."

"The richest man in Vezelay. Lionel Jourdan?"

"Probably. Alexandra told me once that they've owned the place since the early nineteen forties."

"The piece of paper," Jan mused, "could be a postage stamp."

"You're jumping to conclusions," Eric objected. "It could be a letter or a will. And considering that Jacques had already obtained funds for an expensive trip, you can't rule blackmail out."

"I still like the idea of a stamp," Jan said. "Also, I'd like to know whether Lothaire is telling the truth. Who is his best friend in the village?"

"That's easy. Victor Bris. He's the trash collector,

remember?" Eric said. "You see him around all the time."

"But not on Sundays."

"No, but it's easy enough to find him. He'll be at the café, drinking beer. What do you hope to learn from him?"

"More about Lothaire," Jan said. "Is he honest? Reliable? Did he and Jacques ever have a serious quarrel? How much has Lothaire confided in his closest friend?"

"Not a small order." Eric sighed. "Ordinarily, Bris is a sour fellow, but if I buy him a beer, he may open up. He isn't so close-mouthed when he's drinking."

As Eric had expected, Victor Bris was sitting alone at one of the café's outdoor tables. Since the mere smell of beer or wine turned Jan's stomach this morning, she suggested that Eric meet her on the terrace of the Lion d'Or. "Besides," she added, "he looks as sullen as Lothaire. It will be better if you tackle him alone."

Jan continued downhill slowly. Joel came along and walked beside her for a while, then ran off to look for Tony. Under a shade tree in the lower square, a countrywoman had set up a stand and was selling nougat candy wrapped in clear plastic. Her business with incoming busloads of tourists seemed to be brisk as Jan went by on her way to the hotel.

Under a striped umbrella, Mrs. Trench was sitting at a small table, drinking coffee. On an impulse, Jan went over and spoke. "We met yesterday at the Jourdans'," she said. "May I sit with you for a few minutes?"

"Please do." Mrs. Trench indicated a chair with a wave of her hand.

Naturally, she talked about ballooning. The day was too windy to risk an ascent, which had disappointed the eager group. Several had gone off by car to visit the Chateau Fontenay, and others were walking on the Promenade des Fossés, a footpath that circled the village on the ancient ramparts. As soon as she could politely do so, Jan turned the conversation to the subject of stamps. "I understand you are a famous philatelist."

"Famous? That's a rather frightening word." Mrs. Trench looked more amused than flattered. "Lionel Jourdan overrates me."

"He collects stamps himself, doesn't he?" Jan ventured, seizing the opening.

"He collects many things, all sorts of rarities. But he has only one prize stamp."

"Is it a French stamp?" asked Jan, trying to sound casual.

"You might say so."

"Have you always been interested in stamps, Mrs. Trench?" Jan wanted to keep on the subject without asking, in so many words, what particular stamp Monsieur Jourdan prized so highly.

"Ever since I was twelve years old. Like many children, I had a stamp album filled with worthless bits and pieces from all over the world. I was very keen to have a set of flowered stamps from Luxembourg, and there were a couple of stamps from Czarist Russia that didn't fit in my book. Screwing up my courage, I took them and some others I didn't care for to a dealer. He gave me five pounds for the lot. To me, it was a great deal of money, and from then on I was hooked."

Mrs. Trench laughed, and Jan laughed with her, amused at the Englishwoman's use of American slang.

"I'm fascinated by the way rare stamps turn up all over the world," continued Mrs. Trench. "Liverpool, Berlin, Nairobi, New York, Sydney. In unexpected spots like Fort Lauderdale and Utica in the States. Now I find out that Lionel Jourdan has one in this tiny French village of Vezelay."

Taking advantage of this turn in the conversation, Jan said, "I've been wondering whether Jacques Frechette—he was my mother's uncle—could possibly have sold that stamp to Monsieur Jourdan?"

"Was he a collector?"

"Not that I know of."

"Frechette. Frechette. The name has a familiar ring."

"He was murdered, back in 1948, right in the cottage we're living in this summer," Jan told her.

"Forty-eight? Interesting. In 1947," Mrs. Trench said, "my parents gave me a trip to France as my eighteenth birthday present, so that I could improve my accent. I spent a month at a lovely old house in Fontette, a village near here. Our balloons went right over it the other day!"

Looking up at the cloudy sky, Mrs. Trench seemed lost in thought for a minute or two. "Frechette," she repeated. "Now I remember. He was a little man, thin-haired and skinny. I was asking for some special-issue stamps at the Vezelay post office, and he came up to me on the street right afterward, saying that he had some stamps he'd like to sell."

"Did you buy any?"

"No. At the time I found him rather frightening, although I dare say he was harmless enough. He showed me a few covers, very old ones he said he'd found in the attic."

"Covers?" Jan asked.

"Envelopes, with stamps attached. Often they're more valuable than single stamps, but not always."

"Goodness, there must be a lot to learn!"

"There is," agreed Mrs. Trench, "but learning is fun, when you're interested. At the time, I knew very little about the value of stamps with errors, or with upside-down postmarks, or with individually engraved lettering."

Jan was beyond her depth. "And now you're into ballooning," she said with admiration.

"Only as a sport. Stamps have been my career."

Eric was coming across the cobblestones toward the hotel, and Jan waved to him. "Mrs. Trench has been giving me a quick course in stamp collecting," she told him when he came up. "Once, when she was a girl, she met mother's Uncle Jacques!"

As she repeated the story, Mrs. Trench remembered one more fact. "He kept wanting me to look at some Mauritius stamps, but at the time the name meant nothing to me."

"I've been wondering where it is," Eric admitted.

"It's a small island, owned by France at one time, south of the Seychelles in the Indian Ocean. Comparatively little mail was sent from there, because it was merely a port of call for whaling ships. Some Mauritius stamps that have survived are poorly engraved, but their rarity is the thing that matters. I own a couple worth a hundred pounds or so."

A hundred pounds! Jan's sketchy arithmetic came up with $250. "That's a lot of money."

"Not as much money as it cost Jacques Frechette to take that trip around the world," said Eric.

Jan stifled a gasp, with an increasing feeling that they had stumbled on a web of facts too closely woven to be coincidental. Mrs. Trench had been approached by Jacques Frechette in the summer of 1947. In the fall, he had left for his global tour. A year later he returned, and within a couple of months he was dead.

"It's got to be postage stamps," said Jan, thinking of the treasure in the attic and forgetting that Mrs. Trench must be mystified by such a remark.

To her surprise, the Englishwoman laughed. "If the treasure still exists, I think you've made the right deduction."

Jan was dumbfounded. "How do you know about it?"

"Tony and I are quite well acquainted."

"Of course!" Jan groaned.

"An interesting lad, your brother. He has a knack with people."

"I agree," said Eric to Mrs. Trench. "Since he seems to have filled you in on the background of this affair, how would you proceed from this point on?"

"If I weren't leaving tomorrow, I'd try to find out from Lionel Jourdan when and from whom he bought the stamp he positively gloats over. He showed it to me the day of the garden party, knowing I'd be envious." Mrs. Trench chuckled. "Also knowing it was totally out of my price range."

"Would Alexandra know?" Eric wondered.

"I doubt it. Lionel is closemouthed about his extravagances, and Alexandra strikes me as a woman with interests of her own."

"Yet Monsieur Jourdan likes to show off his choice pieces," Jan mused.

"It's worth a try," suggested Mrs. Trench lightly.

"Suppose we find that the stamp was bought from Jacques Frechette?" asked Jan.

"Then I'd search the attic with a fine-tooth comb for others, my dear girl. Look for loose floorboards, for false bottoms to trunks and chests. Try to imagine, if you were hiding something important, where you'd put it." Mrs. Trench sighed lingeringly. "If business wasn't calling me back to London, I'd love to stay and help!"

"Let's keep on supposing," suggested Eric. "If Jan—or anyone—does turn up some more old stamps, should they be sent to you or some other expert for appraisal?"

"There's a man right in Avallon who could handle the job." Mrs. Trench took a scrap of paper from her handbag and wrote down an address. "We do business together, and he'd know if there's anything that would interest me."

She glanced toward the hill, down which a trio of her companion balloonists were strolling. "Isn't this a remarkable village?" she asked, changing the subject abruptly. "Envision a mass of weary pilgrims climbing that hill in the Middle Ages. Ten thousand people living here, and thousands more being lodged and fed. It boggles the imagination!"

13

Eric and Jan started toward home, thinking over all they had learned.

"What about your conversation with Victor Bris?" Jan asked finally.

Eric yawned. "That will keep. A washout, practically. Besides, I'm tired of talking. Tell you what, let's go for a swim." He looked up at the sky, where the clouds were moving rapidly toward the west. "I know a neat place beyond the Two Bridges. Pop's busy at the typewriter. I'm sure I could borrow the car."

He spoke so naturally that Jan's reaction didn't surface for several seconds. Then she realized that for the first time Eric was suggesting that they go out together, and she was delighted.

"Could you make up some sandwiches? I'll bring some fruit and something cold to drink."

"Jambon et fromage?" asked Jan, exercising her scanty French.

"Sounds good. I'll pick you up in half an hour."

Eric didn't race the French drivers along the road to St. Père, nor did he have much to say to Jan, who sat quietly by his side, filled with an increasing glow. She too was tired of talking and speculating, wanting only to savor every moment of this unexpected and pleasant interval.

The road past the Église Notre-Dame, as the church in St. Père was rather grandly called, was crowded as usual with the parked cars of sightseers. Through the open door of the cobbler's shop, Jan could see the *sabot* maker at work, even though it was Sunday. She supposed that during the tourist season artisans seldom shut up shop. Money had to be made whenever the time, like the grain in the fields, was ripe.

The picnic spot Eric chose was very quiet and remote, at least a mile and a half beyond the bridges. There was a grassy bank, a pool of deep water, a pair of mockingbirds, and a turtle sunning itself on a crumbling log.

"*Voilà*!" Eric said.

He stripped off his shirt and hit the water in a

long, flat dive, meeting the icy shock head on. Jan, not to be outdone, followed, and they swam and played water tag for ten minutes or so, then sat in the grass on beach towels, drying off.

"Let's eat," Eric proposed after a while.

The ham and cheese, tucked into split sections of long *baguettes,* were plentiful and filling. The pears and peaches Eric had brought along were warmed by the Burgundy sun, which was again shining comfortably. Juice dribbled down Jan's chin until she washed it away with river water.

The beach towels were wet, so Eric stretched out on the grass, and Jan sat beside him, drying her hair by running a wide-toothed comb through it to untangle the strands.

Eric's eyes drowsily followed the movements of her hands and arms. "Nice," he murmured.

"Yes, it's a lovely afternoon."

"I didn't mean that. I mean it's nice watching you."

Jan smiled. "It's nice seeing you so relaxed." She put down the comb and said, "Know something? I'm beginning to feel quite comfortable with you."

"Weren't you always?"

"Certainly not. You were very disconcerting."

"Was I?" Eric heaved a surprised sigh. "Just overreacting."

To me? Jan wondered. Or to someone else? She didn't ask and resumed combing her hair.

After a long silence, Eric said, "I guess I've got to get smarter about girls."

Jan lifted the fall of hair off her neck and flung it forward so that it concealed her eyes. "Or perhaps more understanding?"

"Understanding?" Eric hooted, startling a couple of crows, which flew away, screaming "Uh-uh, uh-uh, uh-uh" very negatively. Raising himself on one elbow, he said, "I was too understanding."

Jan waited, trying to betray no emotion, until he started to talk again.

"You see, there was this girl in Paris. Danielle. Nifty figure, nifty dresser. We sat next to each other in a couple of classes. Then we started dating. I was mad for her."

Jan noticed the use of the past tense.

"We went around together for a year almost, and I thought we had a really good relationship going. That was where I was not very smart."

Jan's interest quickened, but she didn't interrupt.

"We had a sort of understanding, but we agreed we should graduate before getting married."

It went that far? Jan remembered her mother's belief that Eric had been badly hurt.

"We weren't actually engaged, not with a ring and all that jazz, but we only saw each another. At least, so I thought. Then, one night, Danielle told me almost casually that she'd met this guy in the dress business and that she was going to quit school and be a fashion model. I was stunned, but that wasn't all. In almost the next breath, she said, 'He wants me to marry him.' "

Eric continued furiously. "There ought to be a law against men like that! That guy's nearly forty years old, and Danielle's only eighteen." As he spoke, Eric's voice dropped to a weary monotone. "The wedding was the first of June."

Jan had stopped combing her hair long before. She sat tense and silent, her eyes swimming with tears of sympathy. "Oh, Eric, I'm so very sorry. I never dreamed—"

With a shrug, Eric asked, "Why should you? I don't know why I spilled the whole sad story. It has nothing to do with you."

But in a way it has, Jan thought, because it answers all my questions. "No wonder you've been off girls," she said. "I suppose you're afraid to trust one of them ever again. Even me."

Eric managed a feeble grin. "I trust you, Jan. Against my better judgment. I even like you."

Trying to keep her pleasure from showing, Jan got to her feet, shivering or trembling, she couldn't tell which. "Careful, Eric," she warned. "That's where it all starts."

Jan kept the conversation light as they packed up their gear and walked back to the car. She realized that Eric was emotionally drained, but that confiding in her had been good for him, a step toward recovery. Now he needed easy-going companionship, but no stress.

When they reached St. Père, the cobbler's shop was still open, and Jan decided to go in and price some *sabots*. "The orchard is terribly muddy after a rain," she explained. "I sink in over my sneakers when I help Mother hang up clothes."

"So now you're going to be the rich peasant type?" Eric asked.

"Change rich to poor, and you have it."

The shoemaker recognized Jan and called, "*Bonjour, mademoiselle*," with a snaggle-toothed grin. Obviously, he had remembered their first encounter.

Jan tried on two pairs of wooden shoes he handed down to her and walked around in the sawdust, trying to keep her heels from slipping.

"It gets easier with practice," Eric told her. "Or so the man says."

Selecting the pair that fit best, Jan asked the price. It seemed reasonable enough, and she counted out the francs carefully, while the shoemaker repeated the humorous ploy of Jan's previous visit. Again he reached for the biggest *sabots* on his shelves. "*Pour votre fiancé!*"

Not in the least disconcerted by the wink the old fellow gave Jan, Eric took the huge wooden shoes and leaned down to slip them on over his sandals.

They looked enormous and ridiculous. He laughed and said to Jan, "They'd fit Lionel Jourdan."

"Ah, oui, Monsieur Jourdan," agreed the shoemaker, recognizing the name immediately. He took the shoes back from Eric, turned them upside down, and launched into a flood of descriptive French.

"What under the sun was he saying?" Jan asked Eric, as they walked back to the car.

"He makes *sabots* for Lionel Jourdan, big ones like those, but he always has to tack rubber grips to the bottoms, because Monsieur Jourdan claims the wood slips on the gravel roads near his house."

Jan shut her eyes tight for a split second, then opened them again. "That footprint in the attic. Eric, wait!"

She clutched his hand and dragged him back to the shop, saying, "We've got to measure those big *sabots*!"

Eric burst out laughing. "Jan, you're not suggesting—Lionel Jourdan stamping around in your attic? Ridiculous!"

"Not so ridiculous," Jan persisted. "He's a very determined man, and he could have been looking for something very special."

Dubiously Eric shook his head. "But why, when he had every opportunity to search the house during the thirty-two years it stood empty, would he wait until the new owners moved in?"

Jan didn't answer until she had persuaded the

mystified *sabotier* to allow her to measure the length and width of his largest pair of wooden shoes. Then she reminded Eric that her family hadn't moved into the cottage when the attic was first entered.

"The car was parked near the Centre," she said, "where we were staying with the Sisters, so he wouldn't have known we were around yet. We heard the prowler at the end of our picnic supper under the grape arbor."

Eric continued to shake his head. "Pretty soon you'll be claiming Lionel pushed you off the parapet."

"No, I don't think he did," Jan replied seriously. "I can't believe it was the mayor or the priest either. They just don't seem the type. But it could have been Lothaire Dubois or Victor Bris."

"By the way, his name is Victor Louis, and Jacques Frechette apparently called him Lou."

"Another *L*. I can't bear it!" Jan complained. "Could he have been the one Jacques confided in?"

"I doubt it, but he could have stirred the villagers up. If he knew just enough but not too much, he'd have a high old time feeding their suspicions."

Jan moaned in exasperation. "Everything gets more complicated." Then she asked quickly, "Eric, has Monsieur Jourdan always walked with a cane?"

"No. Alexandra told me he hurt his knee a few weeks ago. Fluid on it, or something. He's being extra careful while it heals."

"A few weeks ago? You don't know exactly when?"

"No, I don't. Give up," he advised Jan, as they neared Vezelay. "It's been a great afternoon. Don't spoil it with detective games."

14

Back at the cottage, Jan and Eric found their two younger brothers sitting under a cherry tree, a dishpan of water between them, soaking postage stamps from old envelopes.

"Where did you get those?" asked Eric.

"Stop right this minute!" squealed Jan in dismay.

"Why?" asked Tony blandly.

"Don't you know that stamps attached to envelopes are often worth more than single stamps?" asked Jan, airing her newfound knowledge.

"Really?" Tony looked interested. "Who said?"

"Where did you get those?" Eric asked again, before Jan could reply.

"I brought them over," Joel admitted quietly. "You said you were finished reading the letters. They were cluttering up the house."

"My orderly brother!" Eric was vexed. "Play with your own toys, not mine."

"I didn't think you'd care, Eric. Honestly!" Joel was contrite. "I've got the letters put aside, and the stamps aren't worth anything."

"How do you know?" Jan looked at Tony rather than at Joel. "You could be destroying something important."

"We know," said Tony in a superior manner, "because we showed them to the balloon lady."

"Mrs. Trench?"

"Yep. She looked them over carefully and said they'd be good for a stamp album, but that was all. Then she paid us five francs for a postcard, but I think it was just so we could buy a *goûter*."

"Speak English," said Jan.

"A snack," Tony answered. "An ice-cream cone, actually." He licked his lips.

Jan looked down at the stamps floating in the water, then turned to Eric and spread her hands. "Well, Mrs. Trench knows what she's talking about, and I presume she's honest."

Eric nodded and moved toward the cottage with Jan. They went through the back door and climbed the ladder to the attic. Kneeling on the floor, Jan compared the outline of the *sabot* with the crayon marks she had made earlier. The width matched exactly, but the wooden shoe was longer by a couple of inches. She was puzzled.

Rocking back on her heels, she looked up at Eric, and he knelt beside her. "Of course," he said, "a tacked-on rubber sole wouldn't reach all the way to the upturned toe." Then he took a long breath of pure astonishment. "Well, I'll be darned."

"It fits then?" Jan's heart pounded excitedly.

"The shoe fits, that's quite clear, but not Lionel Jourdan's involvement. He's too reputable a man to be playing shady games."

Jan didn't argue. Instead, she looked around the attic and said, "Now we should follow Mrs. Trench's suggestion and turn this place inside out!" She looked ready to begin that very minute, but the creak of the garden gate and her parents' approaching voices reminded her that the afternoon light was fading fast.

"I'll start tomorrow morning," she decided. Then she added wistfully, "I suppose you have to work."

"Monday always comes." Eric got to his feet and looked down again at the crayon marks on the floor. "Jan, I wouldn't talk about this discovery until—Well, just until."

Jan looked dubious. "What can I tell the family?"

"Can't you say you'll finish cleaning the attic?" Eric looked around at Tony's accumulated rubble. "That makes sense."

The next morning Jan did as he suggested, and although this spurt of housewifely enthusiasm surprised her mother, she lent equipment and encouragement. Tony, however, considered the project silly. "The attic's clean enough for me," he said. "After all, it's going to be my room if the carpenter ever comes to cut out that window."

Despite the second break-in, Tony insisted he still was not scared of the attic. Jan was, however. As she climbed the ladder she was thinking, night or day, this place gives me the creeps. She wished she were down in the orchard, helping her mother hang up laundry. Instead, Mrs. Nelson had borrowed Jan's new *sabots* and was doing the job alone. The day was overcast and breezy, a north wind animating the flapping clothes in a manic dance and sweeping into the attic to swirl dust from the rafters. Jan coughed spasmodically and wondered whether she was setting off on a wild goose chase.

Nevertheless, she persevered, working around the room clockwise. She wiped out each drawer of the rickety bureau, turning them upside down, making certain there were no false bottoms, and checking for possible hiding places in which a paper or an envelope might be taped.

When it was clean but empty, she looked at the piece of furniture reprovingly, then went on to the trunks. The first still smelled faintly of mothballs. The blankets it had housed for more than thirty years were being used on the beds downstairs. No hidden recesses here, no clothing tray to be tampered with. Just the dust of ages and a few pellets of mouse dirt. Jan wrinkled her nose in disgust.

The second trunk was more productive. Although Jan had failed to return Armand's copybooks, there were a few mildewed leather-bound books and the family Bible. She went through the Bible systematically, riffling the pages a few at a time. Toward the end of the New Testament she came across another faded picture of Jacques Frechette. A duplicate of the one on the mantel, with a gray cardboard mat backed by brown paper, Jan noticed that a number of words in Jacques' characteristic scrawl slanted across the back.

She carried the photograph to the light and deciphered the words *"mon cher frère."* Another word, quite clearly written, seemed to be in English. *Legs.* The remarks were probably of little interest, but worth asking Eric to translate. With the picture she put the brittle pages of the 1948 *Paris Soir,* rescued from the blanket trunk on that distant day when she and Tony had started to clean the attic.

The leather-bound books, when examined, rewarded Jan only by an unpleasant odor of mildew. She continued to work her way around the room, cleaning as she went. The water in her bucket turned from gray to black, and with every passing hour she became more discouraged.

There were no loose boards in the floor, none that had been tampered with or nailed down in an odd manner. The rafters were dirty, but when swept with a brush rewarded her with no pennies from heaven. With a flashlight, she inspected every dark nook and cranny, a lonely job and time-consuming. Not until midafternoon did Jan convince herself that there was nothing she had overlooked.

Tony would have a clean bedroom, Jan thought ruefully. The attic smelled of Clorox and soap. No mustiness remained. She picked up the newspaper and photograph, taking them downstairs. Lean pickings from a long day's work!

Her mother, with a market basket on her arm, was ready to go out. "I'm going to the *charcuterie,*" she said. "Then I may stop by to thank Alexandra for her lovely party."

Jan nodded wearily, wishing she felt as crisp and fresh as her mother looked. "Mrs. Trench left today, I believe," she said idly. "Poor Eric. His chances of getting a balloon ride look pretty slim. He still acts optimistic, though."

"Eric does seem in better spirits these days."

Jan grinned. "He's beginning to tolerate me." She said nothing more, but knew that her mother understood.

"I'm glad." Mrs. Nelson started off, calling over her shoulder, "Doug's off somewhere with Jim Stockton. He'll be back about six."

Just after five thirty, Eric stopped by on his way home from work at the Jourdans. "I've got some news," he said, when Jan appeared in the doorway. "I stole a march on you! Since I was up at the house with Alexandra, and Monsieur Jourdan was around too, I asked him if I could see the stamp Mrs. Trench was raving about. He seemed quite willing to show it to me, and although it doesn't look like much, I made noises about how interested I was. Then I suddenly got an idea. I decided to use surprise tactics." He paused for breath.

"Surprise tactics?"

"Yes. I just came right out and asked, 'Did you buy this stamp from Jacques Frechette?' "

"Eric, you didn't!"

"Nothing ventured, nothing gained, Jan. I've never seen Lionel Jourdan caught off guard before, but his mouth dropped open—actually! He didn't have to answer. His astonishment was a dead give-away."

Jan gasped.

Eric continued, "After what seemed a very long time, he asked, 'How did you know?' Of course, I had to confess that I was just guessing. He didn't say a word, but he put the stamp away in that little glass box it lives in, slammed the desk drawer shut, and locked it."

Eric looked triumphant. "I apologized, said I hadn't intended to upset him. 'What difference does it make where you got it?' I asked, which seemed to make him furious. Remember that heavy metal tool from the old mint, Jan? He picked it up from the desk and toyed with it as if he'd like to sock me one. Then he slammed it down on the desk, glared at me —still without speaking—and stamped out of the room."

"But why should he be so angry?"

"I can't answer that one," Eric replied, "but some of the pieces of the puzzle seem to be fitting together. Jacques must have been holding out on him—about what I don't know—and, as you said yourself, Monsieur Jourdan is a very determined man. Remember, he must have bought that ladder when he attempted to search your attic. To go to such a lot of trouble means he had a very good reason. Don't you agree?"

"I agree," said Jan, "but I'm also fairly certain all his efforts would have been wasted. I spent the whole day in the attic and came away with nothing, or practically nothing—a couple of crumbling newspaper pages and another dumb picture of Jacques Frechette."

Eric examined the *Paris Soir* pages with some interest, but discovered little. "The sensation didn't last long in Paris," he told Jan. "There's only a small item on an inside page, saying the murder is still unsolved."

He tossed the paper aside and picked up the photograph. "Same as the one on the mantel."

"Cheaper by the dozen," said Jan. "There's writing on the back of this one, though."

Turning the picture over, Eric carried it to the door, frowning as he tried to read Jacques' wretched handwriting on the dark paper. " '*Ne me détruis pas,*' he began, then bent closer, turning to catch a better light, " '*mon cher frère, ton legs demeure en moi.*' Say, this is peculiar, Jan. Very peculiar, really. Translated into English, it reads, 'Do not destroy me, dear brother. Your legacy lies in me.' "

Jan didn't try to hide her disappointment. "Sounds like nonsense. Maybe the villagers are right, and Jacques really was crazy."

Shaking his head in disagreement, Eric repeated the message. "The words sound scoffing, even insolent. The dear-brother bit doesn't seem in character. I think Jacques is holding Armand cheap, giving him the raspberry."

" 'Do not destroy me,' " Jan's voice sank to a whisper. "Is Jacques warning Armand not to kill him?"

"Perhaps. You could read it that way."

Jan bent over the writing on the oblong of cardboard. "What's this about legs?"

"*Legs* is *legacy* in French," Eric explained with a chuckle.

"What legacy? Jacques was poor, and Armand was said to be rich."

"Maybe Armand wasn't the big shot he pretended to be. Who knows?"

"Who knows what?" asked Mr. Nelson, ducking through the arbor with a string of trout in one hand. He held up the catch proudly as he greeted Eric. "Your father knows where the fish live, that's for sure!"

He took the trout to the kitchen, returning to the front room just as Mrs. Nelson and Tony came down the path. Each looked at Jacques' cryptic message, heard Eric's translation, and each had a different interpretation to suggest.

"Looks like Jacques is trying to blackmail Armand," decided Tony at once, although Jan suspected he wasn't quite sure what blackmail meant.

"I think it's more subtle than it appears on the surface," said Mr. Nelson thoughtfully.

" 'Your legacy,' " repeated Mrs. Nelson, as if she were thinking out loud. "Jacques wasn't talking about the cottage. They owned that jointly."

"I think *legacy* is the key word," said Jan slowly. "Could the legacy be another postage stamp?" she asked Eric.

"What do you mean, another?" Jan's father inquired.

Eric explained the Jourdan connection in some detail, while the Nelsons listened in astonishment. "I find it hard to believe," said Jan's mother when he had finished.

"All that uproar for one old stamp?" Tony looked

at Eric in bafflement. "Boy, your Mr. Jourdan must be as loony as Mom's Uncle Jacques."

"Suppose Jacques wasn't loony?" suggested Eric. "Suppose he was just odd or perhaps a little too cocky for his own good?"

So cocky that he invited murder? Jan wondered, but she didn't ask. Her father was getting restless, because the conversation seemed to be leading nowhere. "If Jacques did own another valuable stamp or two," he said, "I'm afraid they're long gone."

Jan wasn't ready to give up quite yet. "We could go through the Bible page by page," she said. "Jacques writes 'Your legacy lies in me,' and I found the photograph in the Bible."

"I'll start!" whooped Tony, and made for the attic, returning minutes later with the heavy book. He put it on the table and started turning the fragile pages one by one, until the monotony of the task led him to turn it over to his father.

Eric looked on dubiously and wasn't surprised when nothing interesting was found between the leaves. Between Genesis and Deuteronomy, only three dead bugs and a pressed violet were discovered.

Mr. Nelson went off to clean the trout, Eric headed home for dinner, and while her mother washed a big head of garden lettuce Jan sat under the grape arbor and thought.

Somebody had been told Jacques' secret, somebody whose first name began with L. Would Eric be willing to confront Lothaire Dubois, Victor Louis Bris, or even the mayor and see if any of them might be able to offer a clue to the hiding place?

That nothing could be done tonight was obvious. Although the trout were delicious, Jan ate from habit rather than with special relish. She went to bed early and slept fitfully, while the words "your legacy lies in me" drummed a tantalizing tattoo in her subconscious. She awakened in the morning yawning and was forced to decide that only in fiction did characters manage to solve mysteries in their sleep.

15

The morning was golden and beckoning. It was the height of the Burgundy summer. The Nelsons decided to drive to Clamecy, a nearby market town where canoes could be rented on a broad, quiet river call the Yonne.

Jan helped her mother pack lunch, but at the last minute decided not to go. "I think I'd rather spend the day sketching," she said. Reading her mother's expression accurately, she added, "Don't worry. I'll stick to the village streets."

"And keep your back against a wall," suggested Tony.

Actually, Jan decided against the excursion because she wanted to be alone. Although yesterday's discoveries might have been crucial, the pieces of the puzzle still didn't fit.

Who had pushed her off the parapet, and why? What did Jacques' taunting message to his brother indicate? A stamp had to be the legacy he was talking about. She could forget antique coins, fossils, all other red herrings. However, the "lies in me" part was worrisome. Had he swallowed the scrap of paper? Of course, that was absurd.

Back to the photograph went Jan's thoughts. As she wandered downhill on the narrow sidewalk, looking for an interesting subject to sketch, she decided the message was more than fey. It must be a riddle that could be interpreted, if only one were clever enough.

Seated on a stone coping, Jan started to draw the houses staggered along the curving street, their roof lines making an interesting pattern against the sky, but her heart was not in her work. "*Bonjour, mademoiselle*!" called a village acquaintance with a rising inflection that was typically French. Jan answered and smiled, but the interchange was without meaning. She was obsessed by a determination to break the code that Jacques had used to tease Armand, and she was getting nowhere. Nowhere at all!

A *baguette* under his arm, Eric passed by on his way home for lunch. He stopped to look over her shoulder. "You should show your sketches to my mother," he said. "I think she'd be interested." Then, on the spur of the moment, he invited her to come along home with him. "I'll build us a real American hoagie."

Only Joel was at the Stocktons' house. He ate a hoagie of his own and half of Jan's. "What's the matter?" he asked. "Aren't you hungry?"

"Not very." Jan looked at Eric and said, in conversational shorthand that was over Joel's head, "I'm completely stymied."

"Me too." Eric looked almost as uneasy as Jan felt.

Her uneasiness persisted. Wandering the village streets, she sketched in a desultory fashion until she felt sure her parents would have returned from Clamecy. On the way home, she picked up the mail at the post office and was surprised to find a letter addressed to Miss Janice Nelson, mailed right here in Vezelay.

On a sheet of stationery from the Lion d'Or was a brief note.

Dear Jan,

I enjoyed our chat on Sunday morning. Tell Tony I'm sorry his stamps have little value, but don't give up the search!

If, by good fortune, you find an early Mauritius stamp, take it to Monsieur Jourdan. I have a sneaking suspicion he may want to buy it, and he'll offer you a fair price.

I should add that it may be worth a good deal of money, so handle it carefully.

Au revoir and good wishes,
Pamela Trench

A good deal of money. How much would Mrs. Trench consider a good deal of money? Jan wondered. Perhaps a thousand dollars? Even five thousand? The thought of such a sum was dazzling, because it would mean so much—so very much! to the family. Jan was a realist, however. She saw it as the legendary pot of gold at the end of a rainbow. Deliberately, sadly, she tore the note into shreds and dropped them in the nearest trash can. Nobody need know. Finding this treasure was a blighted hope she would have to learn to live with, a disappointment with which she couldn't encumber anyone else.

Jan met her parents at the orchard gate. They had arrived before her and were now going marketing, but Tony was sitting at the dining table reading a comic book—in French, no less!—and drinking a glass of water.

Coming in quietly, Jan unintentionally startled him. His hand swiped the glass, and half the contents spilled, streaming across the table and onto the floor, wetting a couple of paperbacks and a corner of the photograph of Jacques Frechette.

"Sorry," Jan said, as she helped mop up. "Have a good time canoeing?"

"Super. Dad let me paddle stern."

Jan dabbed at the photograph's cardboard mat with a kitchen towel. The handwriting was untouched, but a corner of the paper backing was soaked and was starting to buckle. "Hey, let me have a look at that!" Tony said quickly.

With his thumb and forefinger, he lifted the wet paper and started to peel it back. "Don't destroy it!" Jan objected sharply.

Suddenly something clicked in her brain. Destroy. Don't destroy me. "Wait!" she cried, her throat dry, her hands cold and trembling. "Where's your penknife? No. Better yet, we'll dampen the edges all around."

"You think –"

"I don't know. Oh, Tony, I don't know!" Jan was almost tearful with excitement. "It's just a possibility," she said, trying to keep a grip on herself.

Very carefully she bore down on the edges of the paper with the wet towel. Then she tried to peel it back, as Tony had, but the dry part cracked with age and came apart in fragments, Jacques Frechette's strange message tearing to pieces in front of her eyes.

Tony was right at Jan's shoulder, leaning close, and brother and sister caught a glimpse of a glassine envelope. Holding her breath, Jan pulled it gently from its hiding place.

It contained a single stamp.

"Not even a pretty stamp," complained Tony.

"It's not on an envelope either. You never can tell, though. Too bad Mrs. Trench went back to London." A thought struck him. "We could send it to her maybe."

Jan, temporarily speechless, ignored her brother's chatter. She stared at the tiny piece of paper until she was sure her eyes did not betray her. Then she looked up and said, "Tony, we're taking this stamp to Monsieur Jourdan. Right now!"

Jan felt that the little stamp might escape from its fragile prison and fly away in the light breeze. She was also afraid that Jacques had perpetrated a dreadful hoax. If so, she wanted to bear the brunt of it. Then she could break the news to her parents as gently as possible.

Tony didn't argue. He trotted along at his sister's side, talking a mile a minute, and when they reached the Jourdan house he rang the front doorbell while Jan stood behind him, holding the envelope containing the stamp delicately between her fingers.

Since it was the time of day when Alexandra and Eric were almost certainly in the garden, Jan wasn't surprised when Monsieur Jourdan himself answered. "May we see you for a few minutes, please?" she asked in a light and quavery voice.

"Of course. Come in." Speaking English, Monsieur Jourdan smiled at Tony, then caught sight of the envelope in Jan's hand. His eyebrows rose, but his steel-gray eyes betrayed no emotion. "Ah," he said evenly, "so at last it has been found. Now we shall see." Limping slightly, he led the way to the library.

Snug and opulent, the room looked as if it had been furnished wholly by him, not with Alexandra's discreet feminine touch. Monsieur Jourdan turned on a lamp and sat down in the desk chair, then picked up a pair of long tweezers. "You needn't fear," he said to Jan, as he held out his hand. "Even if the stamp has no value, I shall handle it with care."

Meticulously, using the pincers, Lionel Jourdan removed the stamp from its protective enclosure. Then he picked up a magnifying glass and stared through it as though he couldn't believe his eyes. Meanwhile, Jan and Tony stood by the desk, waiting. Neither said a word.

Monsieur Jourdan scrutinized the stamp closely, then measured it with a small ruler. He unlocked the desk drawer and removed the glass box Eric had described to Jan. From the position in which she was standing, the two stamps looked identical.

Five minutes passed before the French connoisseur pushed back his chair. "I should like your parents to come here, if possible."

"They're down in the village," Tony told him quickly. "I'll go find them."

He was off in a flash, and Jan was left alone with Monsieur Jourdan, a situation she found intimidating. "Won't you sit down?" he said at last.

"Thank you," Jan murmured almost inaudibly. As she perched on the edge of a chair on the far side of the desk the Frenchman began to write quickly on a piece of notepaper.

For several minutes he didn't say a word, and the silence grew so oppressive that Jan coughed nervously. She was relieved when she could hear voices in the distance, first Alexandra's, then Eric's. Apparently, they had just come up from the garden.

Moments later Alexandra appeared in the library door, Eric behind her. "Lionel, would you like some tea?"

The question was so casual, so thoroughly normal, that Jan felt she had been pulled back into the real world from one in outer space. Seeing Jan, Alexandra said, "Oh, hello, dear. I didn't know you were here."

Jan tried to smile and managed a brief nod, but she couldn't seem to speak. Her tension was so great that she was reaching a breaking point. She glanced at Eric appealingly as his eyes flicked past her to the desk, where he saw the stamp and its mate in one perceptive instant. He looked questioningly at the powerful man behind the desk, but Monsieur Jourdan was speaking to Alexandra.

"Can tea wait for half an hour? The Nelsons are stopping by in a few minutes."

"Perhaps I'd better be going." Eric also turned to Alexandra, making the suggestion as though leaving was the last thing he wanted to do.

"No. Stay," said Monsieur Jourdan, taking charge of the situation. At that moment the doorbell rang. "Ah, here they are now."

"I'll answer it, Lionel," offered Alexandra, and shortly after she left the room Jan could hear her fluting voice raised in greeting. "Margot! Doug. Do come in. Lionel seems to be holding court in the library. I haven't the faintest idea why."

As the Nelsons entered, Monsieur Jourdan got to his feet heavily, favoring his stiff knee. He shook hands with solemn courtesy and offered them chairs.

Jan had rarely seen her mother look insecure, but she did so now. Poised on a small sofa, she clasped her hands so tightly that the knuckles turned white.

Monsieur Jourdan sat down again, and Alexandra said, "Make yourself comfortable, Margot. Lionel looks as if he has a speech brewing instead of the tea I'm longing for."

His eyes twinkling briefly, Monsieur Jourdan said, "I'll make it as short as possible." Then he sat back in his chair and considered his words carefully.

"Back in 1947 I bought a valuable postage stamp from Jacques Frechette, who had run across some old letters written to his great grandfather from the colonies. Jacques was no philatelist. I could have bought the stamp for a handful of francs, but I paid the top market price for it, which at that time amounted to about 10,000 American dollars.

"Jacques took the money with the glee of a boy Tony's age." Monsieur Jourdan looked from face to face and shrugged his broad shoulders. "He was never a sensible man, and his war injury had addled him further. Anyway, he took a trip around the world and blew the whole bit, as the British say. I guess he had his reasons. Nobody in Vezelay had ever gone around the world, and besides he thought his brother would be envious. Armand and Jacques never got along, especially after Armand began to spend most of his time in Paris.

"In any event, when Jacques came back to Vezelay and quieted down after the excitement of his trip, he let it be known that the cottage contained further 'treasure.' It was rumored that he actually told one or two of his friends what the treasure was, but not where it was hidden."

Whom did he tell? Jan wondered, not for the first time, but she dared not interrupt to ask the question.

"As in any small village," continued Monsieur Jourdan, "the rumors spread. Whether they led to Jacques Frechette's murder was never discovered, but one thing was certain. After Armand moved to

Paris, the cottage was ransacked, but nothing of value was found.

"Then, one late afternoon in June—less than two months ago—I happened to be in the café when *Monsieur le Maire* came in and sat down beside me. He told me that Armand, in his will, had left the cottage to an American niece, who was coming to France to inspect her property.

"This wouldn't have been of great interest if Lothaire Dubois hadn't been getting drunk at the next table. 'Ha!' he said. 'Maybe she'll find that mysterious piece of paper!'

"Piece of paper," repeated Monsieur Jourdan. "My intuition told me it could be only one thing, another postage stamp. I also knew, which many of the villagers did not, that the cottage had an attic, the logical hiding place. Imprudently I decided to go have a look for myself."

"Lionel!" cried Alexandra, aghast.

"Foolish of me, wasn't it? Breaking and entering, actually, although I was just anxious to see whether my intuition was correct." Monsieur Jourdan grinned ruefully and addressed himself to the Nelsons. "Unfortunately, the evening I chose for my childish escapade was the very one on which you arrived.

"I felt a fool, of course, and when I heard your voices I got out of the attic in a hurry, taking a tumble and injuring my knee in the process." He looked at Tony. "I'm afraid I said some rather bad words."

Then he turned back to the others. "It was my first and will be my last criminal act, I can assure you. Crime doesn't pay."

Tony nodded vigorously, and the tension in the room decreased.

"Frankly," continued Monsieur Jourdan, "I didn't expect the reaction of the villagers to your coming." He was again speaking directly to Mr. and Mrs. Nelson. "They never dreamed, of course, that you would settle in. I suppose, after all these years, they considered the cottage and all it contained the property of the village as a whole. Including the possible treasure. But to paw through all that trash!" Monsieur Jourdan shuddered at the thought.

"Ah, well, had it not been for Janice's unfortunate accident in the park–"

At last Jan found her voice. "It was no accident!" she said once more, speaking now to a roomful of people instead of only to Eric.

"I know that, my dear girl," said Monsieur Jourdan to everyone's surprise. "Walking back from Asquins on the lower road, I saw it happen."

"Somebody pushed me," Jan said. "Who was it?"

"Do you insist upon knowing?"

Jan's father spoke up. "*I* insist."

Monsieur Jourdan sighed. "I regret to tell you it was Lothaire, the basilica caretaker."

"And you didn't report him to the police?" Mr. Nelson sounded shocked.

"I should have perhaps, and I would have, of course, had your daughter been seriously injured. But after considerable thought and after consulting *Monsieur le Maire,* I decided against it."

"Why?" Jan burst out. "Why would Lothaire have wanted to hurt me, and why didn't you report him?"

"To answer your first question, Janice, I think that the misguided man wanted to frighten you, not to injure you. Like many of the villagers, he hoped to scare you off, get 'those interfering Americans' away from the cottage. Untenanted, the cottage could still be searched for possible treasure."

"Did he know what to look for?" Jan asked.

"I think Jacques Frechette had given him a clue."

Jan nodded in agreement. "*L,*" she said, and glanced at Eric. "*L* for Lothaire probably."

"To return to your second question," said Monsieur Jourdan, "I didn't report him because I felt sorry for the poor fellow. He had visions of finding a fortune somehow and making his invalid wife more comfortable. A stay in jail would only have aggravated the situation. Instead, as chairman of the committee that is responsible for St. Madeleine, I thought it best to reprimand him severely and to retire him, with a pension that will be paid, not to him, but to his ill wife. Then *le vin rouge* may loosen its hold on Lothaire a bit."

"You Vezelay people certainly stick together," muttered Mr. Nelson, not sure he approved of this arbitrary course.

"We take care of one another, not always wisely," Monsieur Jourdan agreed with a nod. Then he looked down at the two stamps on the desk before him. "As for Jacques Frechette," he said with a sudden change of subject, "the one thing that never crossed my mind was that he had been holding out on me, knowing all the time that he had a duplicate of my little beauty tucked away."

As though he were admiring a fabulous emerald, he picked up the glass box and glazed down at the insignificant-looking scrap of paper. Then he looked at the second stamp and shrugged his huge shoulders once more. When he glanced up again, he met Mr. Nelson's eyes. "How the young people discovered this I don't know, nor does it greatly matter. I will make you an offer for the second stamp, and you may take it or leave it, as you prefer." Leaning back in his chair, he toyed with a silver cigarette lighter. "The value of my stamp has increased tenfold in these thirty-odd years," he said, shrugging ever so slightly.

Nobody spoke. As the tension in the room rose, everyone waited.

"My offer," said Monsieur Jourdan at last, "is $100,000.00 in U.S. currency."

Jan gasped. Tony stifled a whistle. Their father, however, said evenly, "The cottage and all its contents belong to my wife."

"Madame?" Monsieur Jourdan's cool gray eyes did not change expression.

Mrs. Nelson looked down at the stamps for a long time before she answered. "I find it hard to believe that this duplicate stamp is worth such a huge sum. You can't be serious."

"I am quite serious. The stamp is worth precisely that much, but," he added, speaking very slowly and with emphasis, "only to me."

Only to me. Jan pondered the remark. Monsieur Jourdan already owned a stamp so rare it had been considered the only one in existence. Why should he want a second? What did it all mean? To offer ten times as much for the stamp she and Tony had found as for the one he had bought from Jacques Frechette seemed absurd, especially since the value of the original stamp was now bound to drop, not appreciate.

Again the room remained silent for an uncomfortable interval. Then Mrs. Nelson said, "I'll accept your offer," although she looked deeply disturbed. She glanced at Alexandra, who merely smiled and made a small gesture of equivocation. Seeming half-amused, half-dismayed, she did not appear really distressed.

Monsieur Jourdan made out the check on his

Paris bank and handed it to Jan's mother, who looked down on it in wonderment.

"Don't worry, Margot, it's real," said Alexandra with a smile. "Lionel can afford to indulge his whims, even if this is quite an expensive one."

Monsieur Jourdan went back to stand behind his big desk. He picked up the newly discovered stamp with the pincers and regarded it lingeringly. Then, with calculation shining in his eyes, he pulled an ashtray toward him.

Picking up the silver cigarette lighter, he sparked it on the first try and wordlessly set fire to the stamp Jan and Tony had found.

The stillness in the room could have triggered an explosion. Every eye watched the ashes drop. Aghast, Jan sucked in her breath.

Monsieur Jourdan put down the pincers, looked at the tiny heap of ashes, and actually smiled. "So!" he said, as he picked up the glass box containing the stamp he had acquired so many years before. "My copy is still the only one in the world, and it is just as valuable as ever. Now, Alexandra, I think we might all enjoy some tea."

16

Still flabbergasted, the Nelsons sat at the dinner table and picked at their food. Only Tony had a good appetite.

The stupendous check stood on the mantel next to Jacques Frechette's likeness, and from time to time Jan glanced at it in disbelief. No longer would there be prowlers in the orchard or treasure hunters in the attic. The unknown person who had pawed through the box of fossils would soon learn, through the grapevine, that the prize had been found. Who might it have been? Jan wondered briefly. Lothaire Dubois, Junot? It didn't matter now really. Besides, the second break-in was probably quite unrelated to

Monsieur Jourdan's unfortunate visit. On this the whole family had agreed.

Her wandering thoughts returning to the present, Jan heard her mother say, "You do believe Lionel Jourdan is entirely reputable, Doug?" Her voice was anxious. "Suppose he calls his bank and stops payment?"

"I don't think you need worry, Margot. Jim Stockton says Lionel is a millionaire many times over. As Alexandra said, he can afford to indulge his fancies."

"But it's so *much* money. As much as you earn in four years!"

"So now we can all have our druthers," said Tony with a happy bounce.

"All right," Mrs. Nelson said with a smile, "what would you rather have than anything else in the world, Tony?"

"That's easy: A ten-speed bike. We could buy it here and take it home on the plane. Remember those cartons they give you at the airport?" He had it all worked out.

"Done! If your father agrees. And if that incredible check doesn't bounce."

"Margot, relax. You've always been the optimist in this family."

"I can't believe in such unearned good fortune." Mrs. Nelson smiled tenderly at her husband. "It's going to take me awhile to get used to it."

"Think ahead, love, just for fun. What would you

like to do with the bulk of the money? Let me guess! You'd fix up this house and keep it, wouldn't you?"

Mrs. Nelson nodded. "It wouldn't take half the check, actually. We could build a proper bathroom and another big room at the back, which would then be the front. We could lay a stone terrace ourselves, and we wouldn't need heat because we'd only come over on vacations. Some years we could rent the place, but we'd still own it. Our summer home in France!" She spoke breathlessly, then tried to look grand, but she only made the family laugh.

"Jan, it's your turn," shouted Tony, delighted at the thought of a new bike and feeling that his sister must also have a wish come true. "After all, you found the stamp."

"We found it," Jan reminded him. Then she cocked her head thoughtfully. "I have what I want, really. I'll be able to go to college without worrying constantly about money. Isn't that true, Dad?"

"That's true, but you should also have something special, something you couldn't have hoped for."

For perhaps half a minute Jan didn't speak. Then she said, with a faraway look in her eyes. "Maybe, if the college I go to offers the option of a junior year abroad, I could come to Paris and study French."

"Doug, you're last but not least," said Mrs. Nelson.

"I have what I want most in the world. All three of you!"

"Dad, you aren't playing fair," Jan scolded. "If you won't tell what you'd like most, I'll say it for you. You'd like to go back to the university and get your doctorate."

"At my age?" Mr. Nelson shook his head.

"Lots of people do. Besides, you're not so old," said Mrs. Nelson.

"You could go nights," suggested Jan.

"Or even take a year off. I could maybe get a paper route." The check held no real significance for Tony. It could be turned into cash, and that was splendid, but a paper route represented money he could understand.

"You've always said you'd like to teach at the college level, Doug," said Mrs. Nelson quietly.

"And so I would. I won't deny I'm envious of chaps like Jim Stockton. It's something to think about."

Jan turned and again looked toward the mantel. "I can't believe that little piece of paper can change our lives."

"It's an even smaller piece of paper that did it," crowed Tony. "One little old postage stamp. Dad, can we go to Avallon first thing in the morning and get my bike?"

"Not until the check clears," replied Mr. Nelson. "We don't spend money until we have it in our hands."

Tony's face fell. He looked so downhearted that

his mother said, "Couldn't we make an exception this time, Doug?"

To Jan's surprise, her father burst out laughing. "There's the old optimism!" he cried. "Sure we could!"

The next morning, minutes after Tony and his father had left for Avallon, Eric appeared at the door. So excited that he was almost incoherent, he gasped, "The balloons! They're lifting off at ten thirty, and there are two places free. A car accident on the way from Paris. Not serious, nobody hurt, but *two* places! Margot, let Jan come with me. Please!"

Jan looked from Eric's shining eyes to her mother's skeptical ones. A small thrill of fear was replaced by a vast sense of anticipation. To sail in the sky, with Eric at her side! What could possibly be more marvelous?

"I'll give up the year in Paris," she told her mother.

Chuckling, Mrs. Nelson said, "Your sense of values isn't so different from Tony's, darling." She turned to Eric. "You're sure it's safe?"

"As safe as it is to ride in a car from here to Paris."

"How much does a single trip cost?"

When Eric told her, Jan could feel her mother's resistance weakening. "I haven't that much in the house."

"Dad will put up the money for Jan. You can pay

him back later." Eric straightened proudly. "I can pay my own way."

"Mother, there's not much time!" Jan consulted the clock. "Say yes!"

"We're to come down for lunch at a big chateau somewhere south of here," Eric said urgently, when Mrs. Nelson still hesitated. "A place that's privately owned. Imagine!"

Whether the thought of this experience tipped the scale, Jan never knew, but her mother's eyes lost their skeptical glint and she turned to regard Jan critically. "You can't go to lunch at a chateau in those raggedy old jeans!"

An hour later Jan and Eric, Mrs. Nelson, and the Stocktons, including Joel, stood in a field of wild flowers and watched the balloon crew finish inflating the beautiful, cloth-covered bubbles. Eric, about to attain his heart's desire, was full of information.

"See those rectangular baskets? They're made of willow, and the balloonists call them 'cars.' They'll be attached to suspension hoops."

"Every sport has its own vocabulary," Mr. Stockton commented, smiling down at Jan. "The balloon itself is called an 'envelope.' " He seemed to realize that she was feeling trepidation along with growing excitement.

Four people were assigned to each balloon. Very shortly Jan was shaking hands with a pilot, whose name was Ben, and with Mrs. Miller, a stocky woman from Boston who had a generous mouth and fine gray eyes. "Your first trip?" she asked.

"Yes," said Jan.

"You'll love it," she prophesied. "I've been up a dozen times. Even crossed the Alps from Murren, Switzerland. Majestic. Burgundy is cozier, though. Simply lovely from the sky, and safer."

To Jan, the car in which she was to ride looked small and fragile, but she climbed in gamely behind Mrs. Miller and waved good-bye to her mother and the Stocktons with a determined smile. The pilot, who appeared very professional, was checking the ballast of sandbags hitched to the sides of the basket. "Evaluating the lift force," Eric told her, but the mechanics of the ascent remained a mystery to Jan. The various instruments that Eric found fascinating were beyond her grasp.

All too soon the pilot shouted, "Hands off!" to the ground crew. Jan gulped and reached for the basket's rim as slowly, with a slightly rocking motion, the balloon lifted.

Once airborne, Jan lost all fear. Riding in an airplane, she never had experienced any real sense of height, but in the car she had an actual bird's-eye view of the land she was passing over for the first time in her life.

The group in the field, still waving, became smaller and smaller as the balloon drifted south.

Sometimes flat, sometimes rolling, the fields spread beneath in a mantle of color, greens and yellows, buffs and browns. An occasional farmer was plowing or harvesting early ripening grain. A pair of horses raced around a corral, shaking their golden manes. Four puffy clouds, white as marshmallows, cast shadows on stands of summer barley, making them look like brushed velvet. Forests, lakes, rivers, and picturesque villages stretched away to the horizon.

"How perfectly marvelous!" Jan sighed.

"It's everything I imagined, and more," Eric said softly. "I'm going to learn to pilot one of these birds someday."

His eyes had the adventurous glint explorers or seafarers must once have had, Jan thought. From the beginning of time, she supposed, young people had seen visions, and she thought of the men going up in spaceships, their excitement magnified a thousandfold.

The pilot, Ben, took his job seriously. "He's a real expert," Eric told Jan. "To be considered experienced, a pilot must make 250 ascents, and Ben has made nearer 300, all over Europe."

Jan nodded happily and tried to look impressed, but when Eric began to discuss the behavior of a free balloon in the atmosphere she hardly listened. The experience, for her, consisted of the fascinating and ever-changing spectacle, which she regarded through an artist's eye, not an aeronaut's.

Ben, however, responded to Eric's keen interest. He explained the altimeter, a barometer graduated for measuring altitude, and talked about the other equipment in the car—an ordinary barometer, an anemometer, a clock, a thermometer, and a compass.

All this time Mrs. Miller gazed happily down on the scenery, occasionally spotting the van that always followed the balloons to their landing place, and she was the first to point out the chateau at which they were to lunch.

Ben made what Eric called "a lady landing."

"What's that?" asked Jan, but didn't listen when Eric explained how the pilot was descending by means of the combined actions of guide rope, valve, and ballast. She only recognized the skill with which he set the basket down softly in a broad green pasture, where several cows grazing along a fence barely turned their heads as they continued to chew the sweet grass.

Lunch at the chateau was served on a large stone terrace, a munificent buffet preceded by champagne, which Jan wisely refused. Because she and Eric were the youngest in the party, and strangers to the group, they were made especially welcome. The sun shone, small birds flew here and there, pecking at crumbs, and a sleek colt gamboled in a nearby field.

"This is the most wonderful day of my life," said Jan, when she and Eric finally had a moment alone.

"Mine too."

They had wandered off from the others to sit on the broad stone steps and gaze out at the sweeping lawns. For a long time, they were silent. Then Jan posed an unexpected question. "Eric, do you suppose that Armand killed his brother?"

Eric shrugged. "I doubt it. But I do think the murderer knew about the second stamp. It was a crime of rage and frustration. That's the only thing that makes any sense. One thing's sure. We'll never know, any more than we'll know who went through that box of fossils." He chuckled and added, "Although my father says he'd bet on the farmer Junot. He's a fossil freak. Won't let Joel even set foot on his land."

"And he knew about the attic," said Jan thoughtfully.

Voices were calling them to a tour of the chateau, and Jan walked through drawing rooms, a ballroom, a chapel, and an octagonal library. "There are twenty-five bedrooms on the second floor," Mrs. Miller told her, and Jan smiled to herself, thinking of the four small rooms in the cottage and wondering what the owners of this grand establishment would think if they knew she was spending the summer in a house with no bathroom. Then she thought of Monsieur Jourdan's check and felt delightfully rich.

Of the three balloons, Ben's was the last to lift off on the return trip to Vezelay. The wind had shifted providentially, and once more the car rose into an almost cloudless sky.

Mrs. Miller was deeply engaged in conversation with the pilot, so Eric reached for Jan's hand and held it firmly as they floated along. "What a summer!" he said. Then he murmured, "When all I looked forward to was grief."

"Grief?" Jan spoke in surprise. Then she remembered Danielle.

"Don't worry. I'm completely over my fit of jealousy," said Eric. "I think my pride was hurt more than my feelings." He looked down at Jan with tenderness. "Three very understanding women managed to straighten me out. Alexandra, Margot, and you."

Jan pretended to pout. "I don't like being last."

"You're not," Eric said, and right there in the sky, within a few feet of Mrs. Miller, Ben, and a flight of small birds, he kissed her lingeringly on the mouth.

ABOUT THE AUTHOR

Betty Cavanna grew up in Haddonfield, New Jersey, and was graduated from Douglass College, where she majored in journalism. It was during her work for the Presbyterian Board of Christian Education in Philadelphia that she became interested in writing stories herself, and in 1943 she became a full-time writer of books for young people. She holds an honorary membership in Phi Beta Kappa for her outstanding contribution to the field of juvenile literature. At present, Miss Cavanna lives in Vero Beach, Florida.